"Phoebe."

Lord Murray's voice was almost reverential as he spoke her given name.

Phoebe's lips parted in unconscious invitation. His kiss was soft and slow and she returned it, tentatively at first, and then with awakening passion. As she began to feel as if she were melting into his very being, the memory of certain facts intruded and she pulled abruptly away.

"Please, Lord Murray, this will not serve while you are bethrothed to Celeste," she protested.

"No, it will not," he agreed, his eyes still dark with passion. "Not while neither of us are free to follow our hearts. We shall wait until circumstances are such that we may embrace with no shame or guilt."

Turning away so that he should not see the glitter of unshed tears, Phoebe answered as best she could. "Then I very much fear, my lord, that we shall have to wait forever."

Books by Lucy Muir

HARLEQUIN Regency Romance
18–THE IMPRUDENT WAGER
33–SUSSEX SUMMER

Don't miss any of our special offers. Write to us at the following address for information on our newest releases.

Harlequin Reader Service
P.O. Box 1397, Buffalo, NY 14240
Canadian address: P.O. Box 603,
Fort Erie, Ont. L2A 5X3

HIGHLAND RIVALRY

LUCY MUIR

Harlequin Books

TORONTO • NEW YORK • LONDON
AMSTERDAM • PARIS • SYDNEY • HAMBURG
STOCKHOLM • ATHENS • TOKYO • MILAN

Published February 1991

ISBN 0-373-31143-5

HIGHLAND RIVALRY

CHAPTER ONE

"'But when, advancing through the gloom,
They saw the Chieftan's eagle plume,
Their shout of welcome, shrill and wide,
Shook the steep mountain's steady side.
Thrice it arose and lake and fell
Three times return'd the martial yell;
It died upon Bochastle's plain,
And silence claimed her evening reign...'"

PHOEBE HARTWELL READ dramatically to her friend
Celeste Laurence, finishing the third canto of *Lady
of the Lake*. Every morning they read to each other
from the popular poem, and in the seven weeks since
it had been published, they had gone through it once
and were now upon their second reading. Her enjoyment of the beautiful words was as great as ever,
Phoebe reflected as she sank back into the pretty
damask-covered armchair in the Laurences' small
drawing room.

Celeste lounged against the back of a French-style
settee, her eyes half-closed, lost in an imaginary
world.

"I can just picture the brave Rhoderik Dhu, a silhouette against the purple mountains, staring purposefully into the distance. A stern expression settles upon his face as he banishes thoughts of his lady love and dedicates himself to battle. Don't you think the Highlands of Scotland must be the most wonderfully romantic place to visit?" Celeste said dreamily.

Phoebe looked indulgently at her friend as she placed a marker in the slim volume and laid it on the small gilt table next to her chair. Celeste had a tendency to be excessively rhapsodical, but Phoebe had to agree that the picture Mr. Scott painted of the Highlands was most compelling. She herself would like to see the lake that was the setting of much of the poem.

"Yes," Phoebe agreed aloud. "I understand why Lake Katrine promises to be the most popular destination for the ton this summer."

Celeste came out of her reverie and sat up, a frown marring her youthful features.

"I still do not understand why Mama will not agree to an excursion there in July," she complained loudly, hoping that her mother, who was visiting with Mrs. Hartwell in the adjoining room, would overhear. "We shall be the only members of Society who are not planning to go."

Phoebe smiled, knowing full well what Celeste was about, but could not avoid a certain amount of disapprobation from entering her thoughts. Celeste was an only child and accustomed to having things ordered as she wished. She had not taken kindly to her parents' refusal of what she felt was an unexceptionable request to visit the Highlands. Phoebe suspected that Mrs. Laurence was not up to the rigours of such a journey, having suffered a severe attack of the influenza earlier in the Season. But Celeste, with the unconscious selfishness of youth, did not understand the slower recuperative process in adults, and thought her parents were being unreasonably cruel.

Still, Phoebe could understand Celeste's disappointment. Society had tired of the Grecian and Egyptian crazes, and the Highlands had been all the rage since the previous year. The recent publication of Mr. Scott's *Lady of the Lake* had brought the Scottish craze to a peak. One heard people quoting lines from the poem to each other in the street, and many of the ton *were* planning excursions to Lake Katrine this summer. When one was young it was very difficult not to be allowed to join the majority of Society in its latest caprice.

"Are you positive your mama cannot accompany us?" Celeste persisted, having received no response from the drawing room to her earlier complaint.

Phoebe shook her head. "I have explained before that Mama dare not leave London so close to my sister's lying-in."

That was only half the reason, but Phoebe did not elaborate. An excursion to the Highlands would be far too dear, even sharing the expense with Celeste's family. What with the hire of a vehicle, mileage duty, tolls, meals and accommodation, the journey would cost over half her father's yearly income. Probably more, Phoebe concluded sadly. Barristers often had difficulty making ends meet, for they were not allowed to discuss fees with their clients, or to attempt to collect them. They had to rely entirely upon their clerks to obtain their earnings, and even should a client refuse to pay altogether, they were not allowed to sue to recover their fees. She sighed softly, leading Celeste to believe Phoebe shared her frustration over not being able to travel to Scotland.

"It is the worst luck," Celeste complained, albeit in a lowered voice. "If we could go to the Highlands I know we would meet Highland lords and marry them. Imagine how romantic it would be—walking through the heather, the rugged mountains in the background, the lord in his belted plaid, dirk in hand," she fantasized.

"I think a lord would carry a sword, not a dirk," Phoebe corrected. "And I doubt that a Highland lord would ask for *my* hand."

This was Phoebe's fourth Season, and she had yet to receive an offer—from anyone she cared to marry, that was. She rose from her chair and went to stand before a gilt-framed glass, resisting a childish impulse to stick out her tongue at her reflection.

"I wish my hair were any colour but red," she said mournfully. "Red hair will *never* be fashionable, especially when it is accompanied by freckles."

Celeste spoke up eagerly. "That is all the more reason we must go the Highlands. I understand such colouring is not at all unusual there."

Phoebe laughed at her friend's persistence and shifted her focus in the mirror to where Celeste was reflected sitting restlessly on the settee in the background. Celeste had no worries about her appearance. Her complexion was flawless, and her clear green eyes coupled with the glossy black curls that framed her piquant face made an unusual but striking combination. No fault could be found with her slight figure, and her beautiful hands and tiny feet proclaimed her descent from the aristocracy. Celeste was undeniably a Beauty. Yet one of her most appealing qualities was that she was entirely without vanity and never gave herself airs.

Not that Celeste did not have faults. She was rather heedless and inclined to be peevish if things did not go her way. But who did not have faults? Phoebe knew that she herself was rather stubborn and possessed of a somewhat whimsical sense of humour.

Altogether, Phoebe would not have traded her friendship with Celeste for that of a duchess. They had been friends for nearly fifteen years, ever since the Laurences had moved into the adjoining brick town house on John Street. Unlike the more fashionable inhabitants of the area, Phoebe and Celeste did not leave London after the Season, but remained in Town year-round. Phoebe's father, being a barrister, had to stay near Chancery, and Celeste's father disappeared into the depths of the City every morning. This circumstance had led to the forging of a very close friendship between Phoebe and Celeste despite their four-year age difference.

"You do not have so many freckles," Celeste said in an effort to reassure her friend as the moments passed and Phoebe remained silent before the glass. "They do not prevent you from having admirers, in any case. Why, Mr. Arnold calls upon you every day."

"You know quite well Mr. Arnold calls upon me only in hope of encountering you," Phoebe said, turning to address Celeste with mock severity. "You should not pretend to be so unaware of his admiration, nor to refuse to reward such devotion."

Mr. Arnold was a young solicitor who prepared cases for Mr. Hartwell. Calling upon Mr. Hartwell at the barrister's residence one morning, he had spied the enchanting Miss Laurence there, and had been totally smitten. Since that day he had taken to haunting the Hartwells' drawing room every morning in hopes of catching a glimpse of his goddess. He had become rather a joke to the two friends, although there was nothing to cavil about in Mr. Arnold's appearance. Indeed, he was actually quite well-looking, with golden curls, fine features and soft brown eyes.

"Perhaps I *should* take pity on Mr. Arnold," Celeste agreed, "but it is difficult to take someone seriously who sits for a half-hour at a time in complete silence, making calve's-eyes at me. At any rate," she said, deftly changing the subject to the earlier one, "I am just as glad no one you cared to accept offered for you during your first three Seasons. We could not have had this one together had you already been married."

"That is true," Phoebe agreed, going to sit next to her friend and pressing her hand affectionately. This Season *had* been the most enjoyable for the simple reason that Celeste had made her come-out and that they had at last been able to share their experiences. She and Celeste had gone shopping together, attended entertainments together and exchanged confidences about the gentlemen they had met.

Now it was almost June and another Season would be over in a few short weeks, and neither of them had accepted an offer. Phoebe had received one, and Celeste four, which was a small number for such an acknowledged Beauty. But none of the offers had been from anyone either of them cared for. Although they rarely spoke of the matter, both girls realized their backgrounds kept away many of the most eligible gentlemen. Phoebe had neither wealth nor fashionable good looks, and her father was only a barrister. Celeste was the granddaughter of an earl, and had both beauty and wealth, but the fact that her father worked in the City was enough to frighten off many gentlemen.

A footman arrived at the door of the small drawing room, interrupting their separate reflections.

"The Honourable Miss Olivia Atwood," he intoned.

Phoebe and Celeste exchanged quick looks of dismay and resignation. Miss Olivia Atwood, the *Honourable* Miss Olivia Atwood, was not their favourite person, although she was often in their company, and most of Society assumed they were friends. The association was not of their choosing; indeed, Phoebe and Celeste found Miss Atwood's company decidedly disagreeable, what with her superior airs and condescending attitude. Phoebe rather suspected the only reason Olivia sought out their company was that they were the only ones her age of lesser rank who were at least marginally acceptable in Society.

"Good morning, Miss Laurence, Miss Hartwell," their caller said politely as she entered, walking slowly around the perimeter of the room so as to give her friends a good view of her new gown and matching bonnet. "I trust I find you both well?"

"Quite well, thank you," Celeste replied, grudgingly polite. "Please sit down. I shall ring for refreshments." She rose to reach for the bell pull, momentarily turning her back to Miss Atwood. She took advantage of the situation by directing Phoebe a simpering face, which was meant to mock her guest. Phoebe was hard put not to smile at the accuracy of the imitation, though she could not condone such shocking bad manners.

"I hope you are also well, Miss Atwood, and Lord and Lady Atwood?" Phoebe enquired, hoping to distract Olivia's attention from Celeste.

Olivia, unaware of the byplay, seated herself primly on the edge of a gilt open armchair, patting a new diamond pendant that rested ostentatiously against her creamy throat. "Quite well, thank you, Miss Hartwell. I can only stay a moment, but I wished to share my good news with my dear friends before I told anyone else."

Celeste, her face now schooled into a proper expression, sat back down and prepared to endure the call. Phoebe and Celeste knew from the expression on Olivia's face that she had something to lord over them, but even Celeste dared not be so rude as to fail to follow her guest's conversational lead.

"What news is that?" Celeste asked unwillingly. She would at least refuse to comment about the obviously new and expensive diamond pendant Miss Atwood was wearing—most inappropriately for a morning call.

"We are to have an unexpected guest for the remainder of the Season." She hesitated, to create some suspense in the minds of her listeners. "Lord Murray, the Earl of Abermaise," she announced, a triumphant tone in her voice.

Olivia watched eagerly for the effect the unmistakably Scottish name would have on her friends.

Her scrutiny was rewarded, for Celeste made an involuntary exclamation, and Phoebe's hazel eyes widened with interest.

"Lord Murray's father was a friend of my father's," Olivia elucidated. "He wrote to Papa recently, enquiring about accommodations in London, and of course my father invited him to stay with us as long as he wished."

Phoebe glanced quickly at Celeste, and could see that her friend was seething with envy at Olivia's news. Still, she could not refrain from asking the question of highest importance.

"Will his family accompany Lord Murray to London?"

"Lord Murray is unmarried," Olivia informed them exultantly, immediately divining the intent of the question. "He is coming to London for the express purpose of seeking a wife, or so he wrote Papa. He wrote there are no eligible women in the remote region of the Highlands where his castle is located, and that he felt he would be most likely to find a woman of acceptable background in London."

Miss Atwood's announcement created all the feelings of envy in her friends' breasts that she could have wished, although they strove not to let it show and give her the satisfaction. A real Scottish lord to stay in Olivia's house for the remainder of the Season! True, the Season only had another three weeks, but even a day with a real Scottish lord in residence would have been something to envy. Why did such a

wonderful thing happen to a person like Olivia Atwood? Why not to one of them?

"It is odd he did not come earlier in the Season.
Two or three weeks will not give him much time to
select a bride," Phoebe commented, thinking to
herself it was even odder that Lord Atwood had
confided all the personal information in the earl's
letter to his daughter. She rather suspected Olivia
might have secretly reviewed the correspondence.

"He wrote that he did not feel he could leave his
responsibilities for a longer period of time," Olivia
explained. "Apparently he has no close relations to
take over his duties while he is away from his castle."

Phoebe and Celeste were silent, not knowing what
to say that would not increase the look of smug satisfaction on Olivia's face.

Olivia, satisfied that her news had had the desired
effect on her friends, rose. "I must go, I am expected
at Lady Tresham's, but I wished to share my news
with my dearest friends first. We shall be holding a
ball to introduce Lord Murray to Society, and of
course you will both receive invitations."

She went to Celeste and placed a light kiss on her
cheek, repeating her action with Phoebe. After a
quick look into the glass above the fireplace to as-
certain whether her bonnet needed adjusting, she
went to the door, where she paused and turned back.

"Miss Hartwell, you should avoid wearing yellow, it makes your hair look redder. Have you done
as I advised and tried lemon juice on your freckles?

I hear it is much more effective than cucumber. And Miss Laurence, you should not wear green. It emphasizes the odd colour of your eyes."

Without waiting for an answer, she swept from the room with a condescending nod worthy of a princess.

"Ohhh! How I detest her," Celeste stormed, jumping up from the settee as Olivia vanished. She glided across the room mimicking Olivia's walk, and fingered her throat, with a supercilious look on her face.

"Did you notice my new gown, and my expensive new diamond pendant? I know it is a little extravagant for morning wear, but I wished you, my dear friends, to see it and be envious. Papa, who is a baron as you know, bought it with his money. Good money, you understand, because he did not earn it but inherited it."

Phoebe laughed in spite of herself at Celeste's antics. Sometimes it was difficult for her to remember she was four years the elder when in Celeste's company.

"She *was* rather obvious," Phoebe agreed, "but she was also successful, for I must confess I am envious of the Atwood's prospective house guest."

Celeste gave a final twirl and sank back down on the settee. "It is *so* unfair," she proclaimed. "Her mother was already planning to take her to Lake

Katrine this summer, and now she is to have a real Scottish lord staying in her house.''

"It is quite obvious Olivia plans to be the one to marry him," Phoebe remarked. "If she does it will be the Match of the Season. Perhaps it is already arranged, since her father and Lord Murray's father were friends. Although I doubt it, for she could not have refrained from telling us, had it been so. I hope someone else will snatch him away beneath her very nose," she finished uncharitably.

Celeste's changeable green eyes turned as brilliant as emeralds at Phoebe's words. "That is just the thing!" she exclaimed excitedly. "One of us must win him from her. I could not bear Olivia to be the one to marry a real Highland lord and crow over us the rest of her life. I should go into a decline and die," she proclaimed melodramatically.

"It would not be good ton to steal away Olivia's betrothed," Phoebe objected, ignoring Celeste's latter comments.

"She is not betrothed yet. If Lord Murray is coming to London to seek a wife, why, every unmarried girl is a possibility. It would not be wrong for us to try to attract his notice."

"But to intentionally pursue a gentleman—it does not seem right."

Phoebe knew her protest sounded half-hearted. She *would* like to see Olivia get her comeuppance. Some of Olivia's unkind remarks about her red hair, freckles and advancing age had found their mark over the past two Seasons, much as she tried not to let them hurt. Nor had she been the only girl so insulted. Olivia's sharp and spiteful tongue had wagged endlessly about Miss Markham's spots, Lady Ainsworth's plumpness, and Lady Winslow's unfortunate resemblance to a horse.

"What is a Season but a time for us to meet gentlemen whom we and our parents look upon as prospective marriage partners?" Celeste argued. "Lord Murray is no exception."

"I suppose that is true," Phoebe admitted. She was becoming very tempted to agree to Celeste's plan, but should she encourage Celeste in one of her starts? Phoebe knew her mother and Mrs. Laurence relied upon her to be a steadying influence on her flighty young friend.

"Olivia will have a great advantage, with Lord Murray living in her house," she warned, knowing that Celeste did not take defeat well.

"Perhaps not," Celeste said, adding with a rare flash of insight, "for if Lord Murray lives in the same house Olivia must show her true colours sooner or later. Please, let us try."

Phoebe was silent a moment. After all, what would be the harm? She and Celeste would not be the only ones vying for Lord Murray's favour. With the current rage for all things Scottish, every woman in Town was likely to be pursuing him.

"Very well, let us try," she capitulated.

Celeste ran to her friend and hugged her. "We shall do it, you will see," she promised and promptly began to dance about the drawing room floor in her excitement.

CHAPTER TWO

THE NEWS of the Highland lord to be staying at the Atwoods' soon spread throughout Society. Olivia was the envy of all the unmarried girls, and many of the married women as well. Despite the fact that the ball the Atwoods planned to introduce Lord Murray to the ton was to be held in the first week of June, it promised to be the crush of the Season. Everyone who received one of the coveted invitations planned to attend.

The week before Lord Murray's arrival, Olivia called daily at the Hartwells' or Laurences', depending on where she found Phoebe and Celeste. She filled their ears with encomiums on Lord Murray—his castle, his lands, his lineage. Nowhere, it seemed, was there to be found a Highland lord who so exemplified the qualities of both Malcolm Graeme and Rhoderik Dhu, the heroes of *Lady of the Lake*.

The two friends listened grudgingly to Olivia's outpourings. They disliked encouraging her, yet they wished to gain as much information as possible about Lord Murray. Still, it was very hard to suffer Olivia's consequential airs, and Celeste's patience, never the best, was severely strained.

"She will be calling him 'Robert' next, and sending the announcements of their betrothal to the *Gazette* even before he arrives," Celeste said darkly as Olivia left one morning after a call that had been particularly trying.

"Yes, it is enough to sour anyone's temper to listen to her prattle on about *her* Scottish lord," Phoebe said, venting her feelings by giving her embroidery silk a vicious tug. "One could almost hope Lord Murray would turn out to be knock-kneed, balding and fat as bacon."

"No," Celeste contradicted, "the more well favoured he is, the more mortifying it will be to Olivia when one of us wins his affections instead of her. I think Lord Murray will be 'Of stature tall, and slender frame.'"

Phoebe laughed. "I believe you view yourself as Mr. Scott's Ellen with your black hair and fair complexion," she said perceptively. A delicate colour rising in Celeste's cheeks told Phoebe she had hit the mark, but she forebore to tease her friend further.

"We shall find out soon enough what Lord Murray's appearance is. Olivia said he is to arrive this Thursday, and the ball is to be Friday."

"Oh," Celeste cried, her attention diverted. "We must decide what we are to wear to the ball. It is of the highest importance, for it will be the first time Lord Murray sees us. Let's go through your gowns now."

Phoebe assented, dropping her embroidery into the work-basket, and they went upstairs to her chamber. Celeste went straight to the Sheraton-style wardrobe and began tossing out gowns, oblivious to the dismayed looks of Phoebe's maid, Sara. Celeste held various gowns up to Phoebe and studied their effect critically.

"Ivory for you, I think," she finally pronounced, after narrowing her choice to ivory and white. "White calls a little too much attention to your red hair and freckles. Ivory softens them."

Phoebe took the gown Celeste had selected and held it before her again, looking at her reflection in the cheval glass. She had to agree with her young friend's choice. The rich ivory silk almost made her hair appear auburn. Celeste might be flighty in some ways, but she had a natural flair for knowing what colours and styles were flattering to one.

Celeste picked up a green gown and stood beside Phoebe, viewing herself in the glass. As she regarded their side-by-side reflections, Phoebe was struck with a sudden thought.

"Have you ever noticed how similar our figures are?" she asked her friend. "What if," she said slowly, an idea forming in her mind as she spoke, "we were to dress alike? Not exactly alike—the same colours would not be flattering to us both. But in the same style? With our different colouring, do you not think it would be very striking?"

Celeste looked at Phoebe in admiration and a little surprise. "I wonder why I did not think of that myself. It is the very thing. Of course, you must cut your hair if we are to look truly alike."

Phoebe began to wish she had never voiced her inspiration. Celeste had long been trying to convince Phoebe to have her hair cropped in the currently modish short curls, but Phoebe had consistently refused. She felt that to have her red hair in riotous curls about her face in the manner of Celeste's would only call that much more attention to its vivid hue.

Celeste saw the stubborn set of Phoebe's lips. "If our hair is not done in the same style the picture will lose most of its effect. We must be dressed as identically as possible—the same style of gown, same slippers, fans, gloves and hair. You know I am right," she coaxed.

Phoebe studied their reflections in the glass once again. She and Celeste were of the same height and same slight build. If they dressed alike it was true the effect would be much greater if their hair styles were the same, too.

"If we are to prevent Olivia from marrying Lord Murray we must be willing to make sacrifices," Celeste wheedled.

Phoebe turned abruptly away from the glass and tossed the ivory gown she still held onto a chair. "You may summon your hairdresser," she said to

Celeste in the tone of one telling someone to summon an executioner.

Celeste clapped her hands and ran to call her maid and make arrangements for the hairdresser quickly, before Phoebe should change her mind.

ROBERT MURRAY, recently arrived at the Atwoods' town house, briefly checked his image in the square-framed glass above the dressing table. The brown superfine coat fit tightly and smoothly across his broad shoulders, the short cut in the front revealing a striped marcella waistcoat. His fine linen shirt had been immaculately laundered and pressed, and his cravat was simply but perfectly tied, its pristine whiteness contrasting strongly with his black hair. Altogether he felt his appearance would not shame his hosts, although he suspected the current fashions would be more flattering to men of slighter build.

He gave a nod to the valet to indicate his approval. The valet was borrowed from his host since his own had flatly refused to leave Perthshire and go south among the "Sassenachs." Lord Atwood had seemed surprised at this explanation for arriving without a valet, but he had made no comment, only offering the services of his own valet while Lord Murray was at his home. The baron had probably wondered why he had not dismissed his valet for such impertinence, Lord Murray reflected. The English did not understand the fierce independence of the

Scots, an independence that was not lessened by employment as a servant.

"If that will be all, my lord?" the valet enquired, picking up the single discarded cravat.

"Yes, thank you, Sinclair," Lord Murray said in dismissal. He glanced at the small mahogany bracket clock as the valet left the room. He had a full hour before he need join his hosts in the main drawing room. His glance alighted on the bottle of excellent claret Lord Atwood had sent up, and he decided to have a bit to steady his nerves for the ordeal before him. He very much feared the ball *would* be an ordeal, he thought as he poured himself a glass and relaxed into a comfortable armchair. He had imagined, back in Perthshire, that he would come to London, attend a few modest entertainments, select a lady of the proper background, make an offer and return to Scotland, almost unnoticed by Society in general. That, after all, was what his uncle had done thirty years ago when he had gone to London to find a bride. Indeed, his uncle Malcolm was the one who had suggested Robert seek a wife in London when he had decided that at eight-and-twenty years of age it was high time he married. His uncle had also warned him that some of the English might not be overly cordial—that many would look upon a Scotsman from the Highlands as a barbarian.

But Lord Murray had found the situation to be quite otherwise. Upon his arrival yesterday he had been informed by his host that the ball his wife

planned for the next night to introduce the earl to
Society promised to be the event of the Season,
thanks to his being a Scotsman. The immense popularity of Mr. Scott's poem, *Lady of the Lake*, had
made all things Scottish quite the rage, Lord Atwood had informed his guest, a twinkle in his eyes.
He would have his pick of all the unmarried ladies in
London for a wife, he was assured.

Another man might have enjoyed such notoriety,
Lord Murray mused, but he preferred a quiet life and
found the prospect of unlimited adulation daunt-
ing. Still, he could not embarrass his host by leaving, any more than he could shirk his responsibilities
and return to Perthshire unbetrothed. His aunt was
getting too old to supervise the running of a large
Scottish castle, and he had no younger close single
female relatives to take over the reins.

Besides, his people expected him to have a wife to
attend to her share of the many duties entailed in
running a Highland estate, and were becoming im-
patient with his tardiness in fulfilling his obligations
to his name. Only this last week his housekeeper had
taken him to task about it. True, his butler had de-
fended his laird's single state, but only because of his
long-standing rivalry with the housekeeper. Lord
Murray had seen the reproachful look in Balneaves's
eyes that told him the butler felt his lord was forcing
his faithful servant to defend the indefensible.

Lord Murray took another sip of the fine claret
and silently thanked his host. Lord Atwood had been

most congenial, as had Lady Atwood and their two children. He had not known, however, when he accepted the baron's offer of accommodation, that his host had had a single daughter of marriageable age. He most likely would not have accepted Lord Atwood's hospitality if he had known, given his stated purpose in coming to London. It could lead to complications, should Miss Atwood conceive a partiality for him.

Yet Miss Atwood might well be a possibility in his search for a bride. She had the proper background and breeding, and she was very beautiful—tall, with sleek dark brown hair, a fine figure and clear blue eyes. She would not look amiss in his castle by the loch. He shook his head to clear it of his fantasies and placed his empty glass on a side table. It was time to join his hosts.

As the guests began arriving, Lord Murray knew that he would indeed have many women to choose from. Unmarried girl after unmarried girl was presented to him. They all regarded him with apparent admiration, some shyly, some boldly, and some, from their deep breaths and fade-away looks, seemingly ready to swoon. He did, however, notice a few looks of disappointment as they surveyed his clothing. A wry smile touched his lips as he realized they probably expected him to be clad in full traditional Highland attire.

On his part, he found that while many of the women were attractive, none particularly stood out. As time passed, the sheer number of women presented to him caused them to blur together. He was beginning to wonder how he would ever be able to make a choice of a bride when he couldn't even distinguish the ladies one from another, when his eye was caught by two girls standing together in the receiving line. They were of the same height and build, and dressed similarly, but of strikingly different colouring, one of them having red hair, and the other black. Sisters, perhaps?

A Mr. and Mrs. Hartwell were presented to him, and then the first of the two girls stood before him.

"Lord Murray, may I present Miss Hartwell? Miss Hartwell, Lord Murray, Earl of Abermaise," his host said formally.

Miss Hartwell curtsied, and Lord Murray surveyed her with pleasure. Tousled red curls framed a very appealing face across which a few charming freckles were scattered, and a pair of frank hazel eyes returned his scrutiny unabashed.

"Miss Hartwell, I am indeed delighted," Lord Murray said sincerely. "I hope you will save me a dance this evening?"

"I shall be pleased to do so," she replied simply as she passed on, and Lord Murray found himself facing the second girl.

"Lord Murray, I should like to present Miss Laurence."

Not sisters with the different surnames, Lord Murray thought as the forms of introduction continued automatically. Yet there must be some connexion, for it was obvious the girls had intentionally dressed alike. Miss Laurence's gown was of the exact style as Miss Hartwell's, high-waisted with short puffed sleeves and a band of floral embroidery about the hem. It differed only in colour, Miss Hartwell's being ivory, and Miss Laurence's a pale green. They carried identical fans, matching slippers peeped beneath their gowns, and the very ribands in their short curls were set in the same place.

He surveyed Miss Laurence's beauty appreciatively. She had most unusual colouring, with the black hair and green eyes. In the green gown she looked like a sea nymph. As she arose from her curtsy, she fluttered long black eyelashes over her intriguing eyes, and her red lips formed an inviting smile. The minx is flirting with me, he thought, and returning the smile, he asked her to save a dance for him, as well.

"WHAT DID YOU THINK of Lord Murray?" Celeste whispered to Phoebe behind her fan as they passed into the ballroom, following closely behind Mrs. Hartwell as she searched for chairs for the three of them in the crowded room. Mr. Hartwell had already vanished into the card room.

"He is not precisely handsome," Phoebe said judiciously, "but he is well-looking, and his eyes appeared kind."

"I think he is the spirit of the Highlands come to London," Celeste proclaimed. "He looks so strong and rugged and brave."

Phoebe laughed at Celeste. "That is as good a fancy as any, since he cannot be Malcolm Graeme 'of flaxen hair and bonnet blue.'"

"He could be Rhoderik Dhu," Celeste argued, determined to see Lord Murray as part of Mr. Scott's romance come to life.

Mrs. Hartwell found three chairs together in an acceptable location, and the girl's speculations about Lord Murray ended for the moment as they settled into their places. They surveyed the company with interest, for the cream of London Society was in attendance. Phoebe and Celeste did not recognize many of the guests, for they did not often mix in such august company, but they could easily identify their rank and status by their rich clothing and many jewels.

Not long after they sat down, the musicians began to play the first dance, and the friends waited hopefully to be asked to join the couples on the floor.

"Here comes your first partner," Phoebe said to Celeste as she spied Mr. Arnold slowly making his way to them across the crowded floor. Celeste expressed her feelings by rolling her eyes, the action earning her a sharp rap on her knees with Mrs. Hartwell's fan.

"Mind your manners, miss," Mrs. Hartwell admonished in low tones, and Celeste subsided. When Mr. Arnold arrived and requested her hand for the dance she accepted quite prettily. Mr. Arnold was handsome and a graceful dancer, even if he had no conversation.

Phoebe sat the first dance out, a circumstance that did not trouble her unduly. It had happened to her not infrequently over the four seasons she had been out, particularly at entertainments in the homes of the higher ton. A plain girl of the gentry with no fortune, and worst of all, red hair and freckles, was rarely the first choice of a gentleman seeking a partner. She watched the other dancers with interest, noting that all the women seemed aware of Lord Murray's every move. Their eyes followed him constantly and they looked at his partner with envy. Lord Murray had opened the dancing politely, if not entirely correctly, with his host's daughter. Phoebe had to admit she felt a pang of envy herself. Lord Murray was indeed a fine-looking gentleman, she thought, remembering his kind eyes when he had requested she save him a dance. She wondered if he would claim it.

When the first dance concluded, Mr. Arnold returned Celeste to Mrs. Hartwell and politely requested Phoebe's hand for the next. Celeste was asked to stand up with an impoverished young viscount, and as the evening progressed neither of the friends lacked for partners.

LORD MURRAY FOUND HIMSELF in great demand that evening, as Lord Atwood had predicted. He danced with Miss Atwood first, and then several titled women, one of them an exceptionally beautiful blonde. However, he did not forget his promise to dance with the young look-alikes, and directly after supper made a determined effort to find them and fulfil his obligation. The room was excessively crowded, and his task was made more difficult by the many guests who impeded his progress by stopping him to speak, but he finally spied the bright red hair of Miss Hartwell and made it to her side. He bowed to Mrs. Hartwell and claimed his dance with her daughter. Miss Hartwell smiled pleasantly at him as she gave him her hand, and he found her wholesome good looks held a particular appeal among the many bejewelled and silk-clad ladies.

They joined the lively gavotte in progress. He found Miss Hartwell to be an uncommonly graceful dancer. She did not have to concentrate upon the steps, either, and could therefore converse as she danced.

"When I first saw you, I thought you and Miss Laurence might be sisters," he essayed, "but when you were introduced and I heard the different surnames I knew I was wrong. Are you perchance cousins?"

"No," Miss Hartwell laughed, her pretty hazel eyes dancing, "only friends, although we might as well be sisters. We have lived next to each other all our lives, and are rarely out of each other's company."

A lady bumped into Miss Hartwell on the crowded floor as she failed to take notice of her steps for staring at the Scotsman.

"How do you like finding yourself the Lion of London?" Miss Hartwell teased, noting the cause of the lady's preoccupation. "You could not have timed your visit to London better, what with the recent publication of *Lady of the Lake*."

"So you also share in the benefits?" he teased. "You look like a Scottish lass yourself, with your red hair."

"No, I fear London's admiration of things Scottish does not yet extend to red hair. I have been informed a good many times that my hair is 'a most unfortunate colour,'" she said with a mock mournful tone. "Still, I have hope that may change. Perhaps you might inform the guests that red is a good Scottish hue?" she asked, looking at him hopefully. "Should you so inform them, they must believe it."

"I shall be happy to oblige," Lord Murray responded gallantly, realizing he had inadvertently touched on what must be a sore subject to Miss Hartwell. He approved of the way she made light of her distress.

When he returned Miss Hartwell to her mother at the end of the gavotte, Lord Murray claimed his dance with Miss Laurence. She, too, was an accomplished dancer, and he had a sudden charming picture in his mind of the friends practicing their dancing together under the watchful eye of their dancing master.

"I commented to Miss Hartwell that when I first saw you I thought you might be sisters, what with your matching attire."

"Then our ploy worked," Miss Laurence surprised him by responding.

"You mean to imply you dressed as you did to attract my attention?" Lord Murray asked, amusement replacing his initial surprise at such plain speaking from a young miss.

"Of course we did," Miss Laurence confessed candidly. "No doubt you think me shockingly forward to admit it, but I am only being honest. Surely you must realize that every lady present here tonight dressed with the same intention?"

"Every lady?" Lord Murray queried, finding Miss Laurence's calculated boldness diverting.

"Perhaps not quite *every* lady," she conceded, looking at the chaperons along the wall. The figures of the dance separated them, preventing further conversation, but Lord Murray knew that he was going to place Miss Laurence and Miss Hartwell high on his list of eligible young ladies.

After he returned Miss Laurence to her chaperon, Lord Murray sought out Miss Atwood. He felt he should dance with her once more that evening out of respect for his hosts. It would be no hardship, he acknowledged, looking appreciatively at Miss Atwood's generous figure, enticingly revealed in a clinging gown of peach sarcenet.

"It was kind of you to take notice of Miss Hartwell and Miss Laurence," Miss Atwood commented as he led her onto the floor. "They are so often ignored by those of superior birth, since Miss Hartwell's father is a barrister and it is rumoured Mr. Laurence is engaged in Trade. Your attentions will ensure they have a memorable evening."

Lord Murray looked sharply at his fair partner, imagining for a moment he heard a waspish tone in her voice, but her face revealed nothing but concern.

"I am surprised London gentleman are so short-sighted," he commented mildly. "I found them both quite charming. You are well acquainted with Miss Hartwell and Miss Laurence?" he asked curiously.

"Oh, yes, they are quite good friends of mine. I try to include them in the entertainments we hold because their low standing prevents their being invited to many of the ton's functions. But even my offices cannot get them admitted to some places, such as Almack's. Poor Miss Hartwell, this is her fourth Season, and she has yet to receive an offer," Olivia finished, feeling she had sufficiently demonstrated to Lord Murray how unsuitable both ladies were.

So, this was Miss Hartwell's fourth Season, Lord Murray thought as he and Miss Atwood danced. Miss Hartwell was older than he had surmised, for he had assumed her to be of an age with Miss Laurence, who could not possibly have seen more than eighteen summers. Additional years were not necessarily a disadvantage, however. He turned his attention back to his partner, deciding that he was glad Miss Atwood was friends with Miss Hartwell and Miss Laurence, for it would make it easier to pursue their acquaintance.

SEATED IN HER CHAIR by the wall, Phoebe watched speculatively as Lord Murray took the floor with Olivia for a second time that evening. They did make a handsome couple, both tall and dark. Olivia was the only lady Lord Murray had honoured with a second dance, and Phoebe wondered if the distinction had any significance. Although she reasoned good manners dictated that Lord Murray pay special attention to his host's daughter, she cautioned herself not to allow her dislike of Olivia to blind her to the fact that Olivia *was* very beautiful. He might very well have asked her to dance a second time because he had found her particularly attractive. Perhaps she and Celeste had not caught his interest after all.

Phoebe reprimanded herself for the turn her thoughts were taking. Since she had met Lord Murray this evening, Celeste's plan to win Lord Murray's notice from Olivia and attach it themselves did not seem quite so reprehensible. Phoebe had already divined that he was far too fine a gentleman for Olivia. Not every earl visiting the Atwoods' would have troubled himself to dance with two young misses as undistinguished by rank or wealth as were she and Celeste. Particularly if one of them had red hair.

Her musings were interrupted by someone thrusting a glass of lemonade towards her.

"Saw you sitting this one out and thought you'd care for some refreshment," a voice said.

Phoebe smiled at the young gentleman before her and accepted the beverage.

"Thank you, Mr. Atwood, you are most kind," she said. Much as she disliked Olivia, Phoebe had always had a soft spot for Olivia's brother Wilfred, who was a year younger than his sister. He was rather awkward and appeared to be as uncomfortable at social gatherings as Phoebe had been her first Season. She always did her best to put the youth at ease, and he showed his gratitude by often seeking out her company, although he avoided that of most girls like the plague. Females in general he found quite terrifying.

Wilfred turned the chair next to Phoebe back to front and straddled it, resting his hands and chin on the gilt frame, causing further damage to his already rumpled cravat. He surveyed the crowded dance floor distastefully.

"Foolish how they all go mad for Lord Murray because he's a Scotsman, what? And all on account of a piece of poetry! I couldn't get past the first canto m'self, although there was a good portrayal of a hunt. And m'sister! Think it was her idea to bring him here, for all the airs she puts on."

"You do not find Lord Murray congenial, then?" Phoebe queried, curious as to Wilfred's impressions of the Scottish peer.

"Oh, he's well enough. Seems a right un, actually. This fuss ain't any of *his* notion. Just the same, his being here makes Livvy intolerable to be about. She means to have him, y'know. Not that I wouldn't like see Livvy get her own establishment and move away—be much more peaceful. But if she's the one who manages to bring him to the sticking point she'll be so puffed up with her own consequence there won't be any living with her."

"I believe that Lord Murray has a great deal of choice," Phoebe said rather dryly as she followed Wilfred's gaze about the crowded ballroom. "He will not necessarily choose your sister."

"Yes he will," Wilfred responded gloomily. "You know how Livvy is when she sets her sights on something. Wears a fellow down," he said, speaking as though from bitter experience.

"Must go," he said abruptly, spying Celeste and her partner leaving the floor. Wilfred found Celeste's beauty intimidating and her teasing ways beyond bearing.

Phoebe was amused by Wilfred's sudden flight, but as she pondered his words, her face took on a pensive aspect. Olivia *was* a very determined person when she set her mind upon something, and she was quite as accustomed to having her way as Celeste. Still, Phoebe could not think that Lord Murray was a gentleman who could be easily persuaded against his wishes. That was the key, she realized. If Olivia were to manipulate Lord Murray so that he thought he wanted her, and not vice versa, he would have her. She and Celeste had only captured his interest for a moment tonight, but their ploy had been a simple one compared to their more experienced and determined rival.

FOUR O'CLOCK IN THE MORNING, Lord Murray noted in disbelief as he shed his uncomfortably tight cravat and prepared to retire without waiting for the valet to assist him. He felt more exhausted by the night of eating and dancing than he ever had by a day of hard riding and hunting in Perthshire. How did London residents manage to keep such hours all Season without falling ill from exhaustion? He finished his ablutions and got into bed, only to lie awake, too tired even to sleep.

He stared at the darkness of the velvet canopy above him and reviewed the events of the evening. He was certainly going to have plenty of choice in his search for a bride. Too much choice, he thought ruefully. How would he possibly be able to get to know even a fraction of the ladies he had met, much less make a decision on who would make the best wife? Before he had come he had imagined that perhaps three of four young women might show an interest in him and that he would be able to spend enough time with each during his brief sojourn in Town to come to a considered decision. Crack-brain!

He wished he had more time, but he simply could not afford to be away from his lands and people any longer than he had originally planned. Not with the days it took to travel to consider. He would be gone a full month in total as it was.

As he tried to arrive at a solution to his difficulties, he felt sleep begin to steal over him at last, and turned his head gratefully into the soft pillow. Perhaps what he should do was to select three or four young women from all those he had met and concentrate on them, ruling out the others and following his original plan as nearly as possible. That was most likely the ticket. But which four? He slipped into a deep sleep, to dream of all the London ladies dancing past him one by one as he sat upon a dais, clad in full Highland garb, trying to make his selection.

CHAPTER THREE

THE MORNING AFTER the Atwoods' ball Phoebe was rudely wakened from a sound sleep by someone shaking her shoulder.

"Oh, Phoebe, do wake up, do!" Celeste's voice came dimly through the mists of Morpheus. Phoebe tried to banish the unwelcome noise by covering her ears with her pillow, but the pillow was ruthlessly torn away. Reluctantly, Phoebe came to full consciousness and sat up in her bed, pushing her hair out of her face and rubbing her eyes.

"I asked Miss Laurence not to wake you," Phoebe's maid, Sara, apologized.

"It is quite all right, Sara. I know you could not have prevented Celeste when she is determined," Phoebe said with a reproachful look at her friend. Sara dared to give Celeste a slightly reproving look herself as she left the room to fetch Phoebe's breakfast.

Unrepentant, Celeste settled herself on the edge of the bed. "It is near ten o'clock already, and we must make our plans."

"Ten o'clock—we only arrived home six hours ago," Phoebe protested.

"We have little time," Celeste reminded her. "Lord Murray will only be here a fortnight and we must fix his interest without delay."

Sara entered the room with a tray. As Phoebe sipped a cup of chocolate, Celeste ordered Sara to lay out Phoebe's morning gown of blue sprigged muslin that resembled the one she herself was wearing. Sara looked questioningly at Phoebe, who nodded.

"Do you mean us to continue to dress alike, then?" Phoebe asked Celeste, amused.

"Yes. It did come off well, did it not? Lord Murray *did* take notice of us."

Phoebe nodded her agreement as she finished her chocolate and got out of bed. She washed her face at the washstand in the corner, the action helping her to come fully awake. While Celeste waited, Sara helped her mistress into the gown Celeste had chosen and brushed Phoebe's short red curls vigorously. Satisfied with this quick toilette, Phoebe settled into the window seat with Celeste for a good coze. They had just begun discussing how to keep Lord Murray's interest when Sara interrupted.

"Excuse me, miss, but Miss Atwood is below. She insists upon seeing you."

Phoebe's sense of humour overcame her and she laughed.

"It appears everyone has arisen disgustingly early this morning to demand my company. Tell Miss Atwood we shall join her shortly in the drawing room," she instructed the maid.

"Why did you say that?" Celeste grumbled. "We have not made our plans yet."

"I could not refuse to see Olivia when I am, after all, up and dressed. Moreover, I confess I am rather curious as to why Olivia should be calling so early the morning after their ball."

"That is simple," Celeste said morosely. "She has come to crow about what a success it was and the fact she was the only one Lord Murray danced with more than once."

OLIVIA WAITED IMPATIENTLY for Phoebe and Celeste to join her in the Hartwells' single drawing room. She had made a point of rising early, planning to time her advent in the breakfast room with Lord Murray's, and had been furious to find him already up and gone for a ride in the Park with her brother. She had felt, since Lord Murray's arrival, that she had the greatest claim upon his company, and had been no end irritated with Wilfred for absconding with him.

A smile touched Olivia's lips as she thought of Lord Murray. He had proved to be all she had hoped. He was well formed, and his boldly chiseled features gave him a wonderfully commanding appearance. She had delighted in all the envious looks she had received at the ball the previous evening. They had all recognized she would take that prize, she thought with satisfaction.

A small ormolu clock struck the hour, and Olivia looked impatiently at the door of the drawing room, wondering where Miss Hartwell could be. It had not escaped her notice that Phoebe and Celeste had attracted more than a cursory interest from Lord Murray the night before. Given their low social status she could not possibly consider either of them a real threat to her plans. Still, it would not hurt to remind them they could have no hopes in that direction.

She heard steps in the hall, and Phoebe entered, followed by Celeste.

"Good morning, Miss Atwood," Phoebe said pleasantly. "I am sorry to be so long in joining you. Mama is not yet awake," she added as a small rebuke to her guest's early call.

"That is quite all right, Miss Hartwell. Pray do not repine upon it," Olivia said graciously, taking the remarks at face value.

"The ball last night was quite a triumph for Lady Atwood," Phoebe commented politely as she and Celeste sat down. "It was the Crush of the Season."

"Yes, the very cream of the ton was in attendance," Olivia said complacently. "*You* would not have recognized them, but the Duke and Duchess of Albany were there, as were Lord and Lady Miffington. Even Beau Brummel put in an appearance."

Phoebe smiled slightly at this not-so-subtle reminder of her lowly social status. Celeste's eyes narrowed and her feet tapped soundlessly upon the Axminster carpet.

"I notice you and Miss Laurence are wearing matching gowns again this morning," Olivia continued. "Such a charming idea. I think, however, Miss Hartwell, that you do yourself a disservice by dressing alike. It must lead to comparisons between yourself and Miss Laurence, to your detriment, I fear. And what could have persuaded you to have your hair cropped à la Titus! It is as though you wished to call attention to its unfortunate colour. I wish you had consulted my opinion before taking such a rash step."

Celeste, who had been attempting to be on her good behaviour, since she was a guest also, could not let this insult pass.

"Lord Murray did not seem put off by Phoebe's hairstyle. I would have you know he seemed to find our appearance quite satisfactory, for he complimented us both."

Olivia smiled condescendingly. "Indeed, he was most amused by your stratagem, and asked me who the two inventive schoolgirls were.

"Are you planning to attend Lady Clarendon's ball tonight?" she asked, changing the subject. Olivia knew quite well that neither of them would have received an invitation. That they mingled in the Society they did only when she, Olivia Atwood, chose to raise them there.

"No," Phoebe replied, thoroughly aware of what Olivia was playing at and deriving considerable amusement from her play, although she could see the remark had the desired effect on Celeste. Celeste was still very young in some ways. "We plan a quiet evening tonight. We are not as accustomed to staying up until all hours dancing as you are, and shall be quite content to rest from last night's fatigues."

For a moment Olivia wondered if Phoebe were quizzing her, and then decided her words were sincere. She smiled graciously.

"Of course, you could not be expected to be up to the rigours of the Social Season. Perhaps," she said, throwing her a sop, "you and Miss Laurence will plan to attend the card party at Mrs. Majors' next Thursday evening with us? I am sure you will receive invitations, for Mrs. Majors does not discriminate against those unfortunate enough to be forced to work for a living."

"We shall contrive to be present," Phoebe replied noncommittally, and was relieved when her guest, satisfied that she had set her friends in their place, soon took her leave.

"I told you she only came to warn us away from Lord Murray and remind us of our great fortune in having someone of her rank condescend to us," Celeste said resentfully as the outer door shut.

"True, but I fear she does have a point," Phoebe said thoughtfully. "Lord Murray will only be in London a fortnight. If we do not receive invitations to any of the functions which he attends, we cannot very well hope to fix his interest." Phoebe noted to herself that she had gone from viewing Celeste's plan with amused tolerance to active participation. One would not think she was all of two-and-twenty, Phoebe thought ruefully. "Of course, we could call upon Olivia at her home, but we would not necessarily find Lord Murray in."

"Somehow we must think of a way to put ourselves in Lord Murray's company. I refuse to abandon the field to Olivia," Celeste said stubbornly. "The thought of her being the one to bring Lord Murray up to scratch is not to be endured."

Phoebe could not but agree.

IT WAS WILFRED ATWOOD who unwittingly provided the means for Phoebe and Celeste to pursue their acquaintance with Lord Murray. Coming down to the breakfast room that morning he had found Lord Murray already present and persuaded the earl to join him in a ride. He offered Lord Murray one of his own mounts, and Lord Murray's appreciation of his cattle made Wilfred a friend for life. The ride in the Park was not what Wilfred had hoped, however, for they found themselves forced to stop frequently and acknowledge acquaintances who wished to be seen speaking to the popular Scottish lord. After halting for what might have been the thirtieth time, Lord Murray smiled apologetically at Wilfred.

"I am sorry, Mr. Atwood, that my presence is preventing you from having an enjoyable ride. Mr. Scott has a great deal to answer for. Perhaps I should have come disguised."

"It is no matter," Wilfred replied very generously, for most of those who sought speech with Lord Murray were women, and Wilfred's fear of the fair sex had made for a very uncomfortable morning.

"It must be quite a trial to you, to have all the ladies pursuing your acquaintance," Wilfred observed a moment later. He began to say something else, and then lapsed into silence. He tugged nervously at his coat with his free hand, something obviously on his mind.

"I must say, Lord Murray, I cannot imagine anyone planning to purposefully stick his head into parson's mousetrap," he burst out, and then blushed.

Wilfred's look of incomprehension tickled Lord Murray. "I have avoided it for a half score years," he admitted, "but the time comes one must face up to one's responsibilities."

"I suppose so," Wilfred agreed doubtfully. "Is there any lady you particularly favour?" he asked, thinking perhaps he could help his new friend to get the distasteful business over with as quickly as possible.

"Lady Sheridan," Lord Murray replied, recalling the stately blonde from the previous night. "Yes, and

the two girls who were clad in matching gowns. A
Miss Hartwell and Miss Laurence, I believe.''

''Can't say I care overly for Miss Laurence—she's
too prone to tease a fellow—but Miss Hartwell is a
right 'un. Say! Let's leave the Park and pay a call on
Miss Hartwell.''

After a moment's hesitation, Lord Murray agreed.
Mr. Atwood obviously wished to escape the Park and
the many intimidating females he was being forced
to greet. Furthermore, he *was* interested in getting to
know Miss Hartwell better, and his time was limited.

IT WAS A GREAT SURPRISE to Phoebe and Celeste
when, shortly after Olivia's departure, the footman
announced the arrival of Lord Murray and the
Honourable Mr. Atwood. Mrs. Hartwell had risen,
and she received her noble callers graciously, but
with none of the fawning over the Scottish lord many
of her social betters exhibited. Lord Murray was beginning to find the attempts of Society to curry
favour with him distasteful, and Mrs. Hartwell's
simple courtesy was refreshing.

While he exchanged pleasantries with Mrs. Hartwell, Lord Murray also observed the two girls who
had so captured his notice the night before. They
were again clad in matching gowns, and he knew
from Miss Laurence's presence at the Hartwells' that
they were indeed close friends. Miss Hartwell con-
versed easily with young Atwood, sitting protec-
tively between him and Miss Laurence. Lord Murray

overheard the expressions "drew his claret," "lily-livered," and "able with his fists," and concluded the young sapskull was treating Miss Hartwell to a discourse on boxing. Miss Laurence noticed him watching them, and after a quick glance at Mrs. Hartwell to be sure she was not observed, cast him a flirtatious look. Lord Murray pretended not to see and turned his eyes back to Mrs. Hartwell.

"Lord Murray, you do us quite an honour to call upon us," Miss Laurence suddenly commented. "I wager London speaks of naught this morning but the brave Scottish lord."

Lord Murray was amused by Miss Laurence's bid to bring attention to herself. She was obviously a young lady not accustomed to being ignored. He was saved the necessity of a reply by the footman announcing a third gentleman caller.

"Mr. Arnold."

Lord Murray looked curiously at the young gentleman who entered the room. He was clad in a plain broadcloth morning coat, the cuffs shiny from wear, and boots with worn soles. His old clothes did not detract from his looks, however, for he had wonderfully golden curls and delicate features that transcended such mundane accoutrements as clothes. A curate, perhaps? He wondered if one of the young ladies were attached to Mr. Arnold.

Mrs. Hartwell performed the requisite introductions.

"Lord Murray, may I present to you Mr. Arnold? Mr. Arnold is a friend and a solicitor who sometimes prepares cases for Mr. Hartwell. Mr. Arnold, Lord Murray, Earl of Abermaise, who is residing with Lord and Lady Atwood for the remainder of the Season."

The young man mumbled something unintelligible and seated himself on a chair in the corner, resting his chin on his hands and staring with his large brown eyes at the sofa upon which Miss Hartwell and Miss Laurence sat. Calf love, Lord Murray thought, much diverted.

The conversation turned to Scotland, a topic which seemed to be inevitable, Lord Murray thought, but he good-naturedly answered their questions.

"Are the Highlands as beautiful as Mr. Scott describes them?" Miss Laurence asked, her intriguing green eyes sparkling with interest. "Rugged purple mountains in the background with thick forests of beech and oak and shining lakes?"

"Yes, so much of the Highlands appears," Lord Murray agreed. It was obvious Miss Laurence had a highly romanticized idea of the Highlands. The scenery was beautiful and, yes, romantic, he had to concede, but it was also harsh and uncompromising. It was not a country for the faint of heart.

"Why did you not wear a belted plaid?" Miss Laurence further dared to enquire. "You disappointed half of London by appearing at the ball last night in ordinary evening dress.''

Mrs. Hartwell looked at Miss Laurence disapprovingly for asking such a personal question, but Lord Murray answered with good humour.

"Wearing tartan and Highland dress was outlawed from 1746 until 1785, and by then many of us were out of the custom of wearing our traditional costume," Lord Murray explained. "Although, had I known I would disappoint half of London I certainly would have brought my belted plaid with me to London."

"Even though I understand that the clans were outlawed, I imagine much of the clan loyalty remains," Miss Hartwell hazarded.

"Indeed it does," Lord Murray agreed with this astute observation. "Since this is true, my task as laird is made more difficult, for I am not only responsible for many kinsmen but for many others who have remained loyal to the Murray clan but can claim no blood relation."

Lord Murray found himself very much impressed by Miss Hartwell's perceptive questions and immeasurably diverted by Miss Laurence's naive ones as they spoke. A half-hour sped by, and he and Wilfred took their departure, leaving Mr. Arnold, who had not said a word since the introductions, in possession of the drawing room.

LORD MURRAY AND WILFRED returned to the Atwoods' town house after their call upon the Hartwells, and Lord Murray spent the afternoon visiting with his host. He found Lord Atwood very congenial company, and could understand why his own father had befriended him. Lady Atwood, a massively built matron with a haughty expression, he could not like as well, finding her self-absorbed and overly concerned about Society. Yet she was a gracious hostess and he was thankful for her hospitality.

Altogether the day passed pleasantly, and Lord Murray descended from his room that evening to join his hosts for another night's activities in excellent humour. He made his way to the drawing room, but hesitated outside the door upon hearing raised voices.

"Wilfred, how is it you cannot ever contrive to look presentable. You *do* have a valet," he heard Miss Atwood scolding her brother.

"I looked fine as fivepence when I left my dressing room," Wilfred protested. "I don't know how it is, but it never lasts. Leave a fellow alone though, won't you."

Lord Murray smiled. Young Atwood did always look rather rumpled and half put together, but then he was still an unlicked cub.

"I shall leave you alone when you make an effort to appear other than an unkempt boor. I am shamed to have you for my brother. What must Lord Murray think of us?"

"My appearance is no skin off your nose," Wilfred retorted. "He ain't likely to reject you because my cravat ain't perfect. More likely to because of your own ill temper, once he gets to know you."

Lord Murray felt the conversation was becoming rather too personal and entered the room rather noisily to give warning of his approach. Miss Atwood turned to him with a welcoming smile, all traces of ill humour removed from her voice and aspect.

"Good evening Lord Murray. I expect my parents will be down shortly."

Wilfred looked relieved to see Lord Murray enter and took the opportunity to move to the opposite side of the room.

Lord Murray politely devoted his attention to Miss Atwood, but the conversation he had overheard rang a warning bell. This was what he had feared might happen. If Miss Atwood were indeed trying to attach his interest, living in her home could be awkward. But then the argument could have been no more than a sibling squabble. Brothers and sisters were likely to accuse each other of anything when quarrelling.

Not that he did not consider Miss Atwood a possibility in his search for a bride, he thought, appreciating her appearance this evening in a speedwell-blue gown that matched the colour of her eyes. Her dark brown hair glistened in the candlelight, and the silk of her gown shimmered over the soft rise and fall of her breasts. She smiled charmingly at his evident admiration, revealing perfect white teeth.

Yes, Lord Murray thought, Miss Atwood would be one of his "candidates." He had decided his idea of the previous night to narrow his choices down to three or four ladies and try to get to know them was the best route he could take. With Lady Sheridan, Miss Hartwell and Miss Laurence, that would make four. Tonight he would try to spend some time with each. Lord and Lady Atwood entered the room, breaking off his train of thought, and they departed for a ball.

AT THE BALL THAT EVENING Lord Murray searched for the other three women, but although he espied Lady Sheridan, he could find neither Miss Hartwell nor Miss Laurence. He commented on this to Miss Atwood.

"Oh, you will not see them here. As I explained last evening, their low rank prevents them from being invited to many functions," she replied.

Olivia was irritated by Lord Murray's continuing interest in her two friends, but not overly worried about it. She was much more concerned about his interest in Lady Sheridan. Lady Sheridan was both beautiful and of higher rank than she. Perhaps it would even be wise to steer Lord Murray away from Lady Sheridan's company and keep him occupied with two who could not possibly be serious rivals. She came to a quick decision.

"If you wish, Lord Murray, we might plan an entertainment which Miss Hartwell and Miss Laurence could attend," she offered sweetly.

"That is an excellent suggestion, Miss Atwood," Lord Murray approved, liking the generosity of spirit the offer seemed to display. "It is very kind of you. Have you anything in mind?"

"Perhaps we might make an excursion to Vauxhall," Olivia suggested, thinking that if she were to invite the right people, she might be able to manoeuvre them so that she could have time alone with Lord Murray. Perhaps even a stroll down the Dark Walk.

OLIVIA ORGANIZED the Vauxhall expedition for the coming Saturday night. After much thought, she decided to keep the party small, including only herself, Lord Murray, her brother, Miss Hartwell, Miss Laurence and Mr. Arnold. Wilfred would keep Miss Hartwell occupied, and Mr. Arnold would claim Miss Laurence's company, leaving Lord Murray to herself.

The party arrived at the Gardens early in the evening and took a Chinese kiosk for dinner. Olivia had decided against a dinner box overlooking the Promenade, for she feared if other acquaintances spied their party they might try to join it. Lord Murray's popularity created certain difficulties.

At first all seemed to be going as she had planned. Wilfred involved Miss Hartwell in a conversation about fencing, and Miss Laurence, seated next to Mr. Arnold, politely tried to engage that gentleman in conversation, albeit with scant success.

But Olivia had not allowed for Miss Laurence's readiness to ignore good manners when she wanted something. Soon after the powdered beef and custard arrived, Celeste began inserting herself into Olivia's conversation with Lord Murray, leaving Mr. Arnold to his own devices. Olivia, exasperated by this turn of events, and determined to regain Lord Murray's undivided attention, suggested that Lord Murray might like to explore the walks of the famous Gardens.

"Oh, that is an excellent idea!" Celeste exclaimed. "Mr. Arnold and I shall join you."

To Olivia's further vexation, Celeste somehow manoeuvered to walk alongside Lord Murray, forcing Olivia to walk behind with the inarticulate Mr. Arnold. As Olivia followed Celeste and Lord Murray down the paths, her only satisfaction was that Lord Murray did not pay a great deal of attention to Celeste, but seemed truly interested in viewing the waterfalls, grottoes, statues and neatly pruned shrubs and trees of the Gardens.

Still, her temper was becoming severely strained, and when they returned to their kiosk to find their party enlarged by the addition of Lady Sheridan and her younger brother, she was practically seething. The

Sheridans had been passing by on their way to the fireworks, and upon seeing Mr. Atwood and Miss Hartwell, had stopped to visit. Olivia was hard put to give a civil response to the Sheridans' greeting.

"I am delighted you could join us, Lord Sheridan, Lady Sheridan," she said, a definite edge to her voice. She saw Lord Murray glance her way and made a supreme effort to control her irritation. It did not help that she suspected Lady Sheridan understood exactly how she felt and was vastly amused.

Olivia tried to salvage what she could from the evening by flirting lightly with the handsome young Lord Sheridan. She could at least remind Lord Murray that there were other eligible gentlemen who found her attractive, and that he should not take her too much for granted. Overall, however, Olivia felt the evening was a total disaster.

IF OLIVIA was less than satisfied with the results of the expedition to Vauxhall, Phoebe and Celeste were not. Celeste, in particular, was almost exultant. She had persuaded Phoebe to remain with her for the night and could not cease talking of the evening.

"We are slowly winning the race—I know it! Did you see Olivia's expression when I invited Mr. Arnold and myself to join her and Lord Murray on their walk? And how angry she was when we came back to find Lady Sheridan and her brother with you and Wilfred!"

"Yes." Phoebe could not help smiling at the remembrance. She recalled, too, Lord Murray's quick glance at Olivia's barely civil greeting to the cool blonde beauty. "I think Lord Murray is coming to see Olivia's true nature, as you predicted. But," she said, a frown creasing her forehead, "we did not consider other possible rivals when we decided to try to win Lord Murray's notice. I believe him to be much taken with Lady Sheridan."

Celeste relaxed lazily on her bed. "I do not care if Lady Sheridan wins Lord Murray's affections. I just do not want Olivia to be the one to win them. Although," she said meditatively, "it would be all that is wonderful if I were to be the one to bring Lord Murray up to scratch."

Phoebe looked askance at Celeste. It was obvious that Celeste viewed the winning of Lord Murray's affections as a game and a way to score over Olivia in retaliation for all the snubs and hurts she had dealt them. She did not appear to have developed a tendre for Lord Murray—it was simply a competition Celeste wanted to win. Phoebe caught herself. *Tu quoque,* as her learned barrister father might say. You are another. Had she not originally decided to try to capture Lord Murray's interest with much the same attitude as Celeste? But something had changed.

"What," Phoebe asked her friend slowly, "if Lord Murray *does* offer for you?" The idea disturbed her.

"Why, then I have made the Match of the Season," Celeste replied, surprised that her friend would not automatically have known this. "I, the daughter of a gentleman who works in the City. Can you imagine Olivia's chagrin?"

"But would you be happy?"

"Of course," Celeste replied, regarding her friend strangely. "Lord Murray is well-looking, kind and a Scotsman. What more could one ask? Would you not accept him if he offered for you?"

"I suppose I would," Phoebe answered as she slipped into the bed beside Celeste. But her reason for accepting would be much different from her friend's. The conversation with Celeste had made Phoebe realize that the plan they had originally conceived had become more than a competition or game to her. If she accepted an offer from Lord Murray it would not just be for the glory of winning.

Phoebe pretended to have fallen asleep, not wanting to talk to Celeste any longer. In actuality she lay awake for a long time, trying to analyse her feelings towards Lord Murray. Was she developing a tendre for him? It seemed incredible, considering what a short time she had known him, but she could think of no other explanation.

CHAPTER FOUR

OLIVIA AROSE in a very sour temper the morning after the Vauxhall expedition. It was not proving as simple to attach the interest of Lord Murray as she had thought it would be. Before his arrival, she had assumed that given Lord Murray's purpose in coming to London, her eligibility and beauty plus the advantage of his living in the same house would inevitably lead to an offer. Instead, while she sensed Lord Murray did find her attractive, he had been careful not to single her out, and she knew she had serious rivals in Lady Sheridan, Phoebe and Celeste. She could understand his interest in Lady Sheridan, but Phoebe and Celeste! His apparent partiality for them she could *not* understand. Perhaps Scotsmen did not put the same value on rank Englishmen did. Whatever the reason, it was creating a problem for her.

Still thinking over her predicament, Olivia dressed in a new yellow striped morning gown and descended to the breakfast room. Her brother was already there, devouring a plate of eggs and kidneys, but of Lord Murray there was no sign. She ignored

Wilfred and helped herself to some toast and coffee, a frown on her face.

"What's giving you the blue devils, Livvy?" Wilfred enquired, noting her furrowed brow.

"I have told you not to call me 'Livvy,'" Olivia said with irritation as she seated herself at the opposite end of the table from her brother. "And do try for some manners, Wilfred. You have spilled coffee down your cravat. How disgusting."

Wilfred wiped at the coffee ineffectually. His sister was on her high ropes this morning, and he knew why.

"You needn't snap at me because Lord Murray shows an interest in some females other than yourself. Don't know about Lady Sheridan and Miss Laurence, but I'd prefer Miss Hartwell m'self."

"You! No lady in her right mind would choose you, not even a red-headed ape-leader with freckles and a barrister for a father," Olivia said vituperatively.

"Don't know about that," Wilfred retorted, stung. He might not be much in the petticoat line, but he didn't care for his sister's implication no woman could like him.

"Good morning, Miss Atwood, Mr. Atwood."

Olivia started guiltily and wondered how much, if any, Lord Murray had overheard. She remonstrated with herself to remember to guard her tongue at all times while Lord Murray was residing with them. She knew instinctively that he would find any disparag-

ing remarks she made about others off-putting. She
smiled brightly.

"Good morning, Lord Murray. I trust you rested
well?"

"Very well, thank you, Miss Atwood," Lord
Murray replied, filling a plate with food at the sideboard.

"Would you care to accompany me to the circulating library this morning?" Olivia asked, hoping
that some private time spent in Lord Murray's company might give her the opportunity to regain her lost
position.

"Thank you, Miss Atwood, but I have already
accepted an invitation to join Mr. Atwood in a visit
to Tattersall's."

"I am sure you could go with him this afternoon
instead," Olivia pressed, kicking her brother beneath the table to encourage him to agree with this
plan. Wilfred, however, if he understood what he
was supposed to say, refused to cooperate.

"Can't, Livvy, not if Lord Murray wants to see
Silverton's bays. They are going up at the
auctioneer's this morning."

Lord Murray had seen Wilfred's wince of pain and
the angry glare he had directed at his sister, and gave
a good guess as to the cause. Atwood apparently decided to get out of the way of further retribution, for
he rose hastily from the table.

"I'll be ready to leave directly after I change, Lord
Murray," Wilfred said as he left the room. Lord

Murray nodded and turned his attention to his breakfast and his remaining companion.

"Perhaps I may accompany you to the library another morning, Miss Atwood," he offered politely.

"Thank you. On second thought I believe I may call upon Miss Hartwell and Miss Laurence this morning," Olivia improvised. "Miss Hartwell asked me for a new receipt to fade freckles last night and I should take it to her as soon as possible."

"Have you been acquainted with Miss Hartwell and Miss Laurence long?" Lord Murray enquired, curious. He had long wondered how such an unlikely "friendship" had come to be.

"Mr. Arnold introduced us this year past," Olivia answered absently.

"Mr. Arnold?" Lord Murray echoed in surprise. He had yet to hear Mr. Arnold pronounce three intelligible words together.

"Yes, Mr. Arnold is acquainted with Wilfred. He is the younger son of a viscount," she added as though to explain how Wilfred came to be acquainted with a lowly solicitor.

Suddenly inspiration struck Olivia. She saw a way to eliminate the more beautiful, and therefore the more dangerous, of her two untitled rivals.

"Mr. Arnold is betrothed to Miss Laurence, you know, although the family is keeping it secret until she has had a Season," she volunteered mendaciously.

"No, I did not know," Lord Murray replied, exceedingly surprised at this piece of intelligence, for he had observed nothing at all lover-like in the way Miss Laurence behaved towards Mr. Arnold, although Mr. Arnold was obviously head-over-heels in love with her. The information was even more difficult to credit when he remembered how Miss Laurence openly flirted with him in Mr. Arnold's presence.

OLIVIA'S NEWS continued to perplex Lord Murray, and on the way home from Tattersall's with Wilfred he ventured to raise the subject. Wilfred was in a particularly good humour, having just purchased a likely-looking grey.

"Miss Laurence engaged to Mr. Arnold?" Wilfred repeated in astonishment, when Lord Murray put his question. "I say, someone has been telling you a whisker."

"Your sister informed me of the fact this morning. She seems to be on close terms with Miss Hartwell and Miss Laurence."

Wilfred opened his mouth, closed it and then with the air of someone resolved to be honest at all costs, turned to Lord Murray and spoke.

"Lord Murray, you've been awfully sporting to me. Maybe I shouldn't say this—I mean, Livvy's m'sister and all that, but, well— Dash it, ever since she heard you were coming to London, Livvy's been determined to be the one to snabble you, you being a Scottish lord and what with Scotland being all the rage this Season. I mean to say," Wilfred struggled on, "when things ain't going her way Livvy has the devil of a temper, and, well, dash it, mean to say don't believe everything m'sister tells you," he finished uncomfortably, but obviously determined to warn his new friend, even if he had to be disloyal to family to do so. "I'd choose Miss Hartwell, m'self," he finished almost inaudibly.

Lord Murray heard Wilfred out with mixed amusement and gratitude. "Thank you, Atwood, I shall keep your advice in mind. This conversation will remain between the two of us, needless to say.

"What did you think of Silverton's bays?" he asked, turning the subject. Their morning excursion ended quite happily in a discussion of the finer points of the cattle they had seen at Tattersall's.

Two NIGHTS LATER, however, as Lord Murray relaxed in his chambers, he found himself recalling his conversation with Wilfred. Time was running out; he had only a sennight remaining in which to make a decision. How extremely foolish he had been to think he could come to London and select a bride in two weeks, he thought self-deprecatingly. Most English gentlemen took the entire Season, and already knew many of the young ladies making their come-outs, or were at least acquainted with their families. He had had no connexions with anyone but the Atwoods. Yet make a choice he must. He could not continue to delay his marriage. He reviewed the four women to which he had limited himself.

First there was Olivia Atwood. She was beautiful and had birth and breeding, but he had observed flashes of jealousy, and worse, malice, in her dealings with her friends and her brother. Nor could he overlook her deceit in fabricating the story of the betrothal between Mr. Arnold and Miss Laurence. Lord Murray had found that the hard and isolated life in the Highlands tended to make his kinsmen mighty particular about a person's character, and Olivia's shortcomings were ones that would not be tolerated. No, Miss Atwood might make a fine London lady, but she would never do as the wife of a Highland laird.

Next there was Lady Sheridan. She was eminently qualified, for she had a stately grace, perfect manners and was of high birth. But she was reserved and difficult to get to know. Perhaps too much so? His future wife must be able to enter into all the joys and sorrows of his numerous clansmen. Still, he would not yet rule Lady Sheridan out.

Then there was Miss Laurence. She was undoubtedly the most beautiful of the four, a true Diamond of the First Water. She did not have the high birth of Lady Sheridan and Miss Atwood, but he put less value on that than other qualities, such as her loyalty to her friend and her eagerness to please. Her main drawback was her youth. Was she old enough to take on the many responsibilities that would fall to her?

He rather doubted it. On the other hand, she had made it clear she found him attractive and would not be averse to receiving an offer. Time would remedy her immaturity. He would not eliminate her as a possibility.

Finally, there was Miss Hartwell. A picture of the red-haired young woman flashed vividly into his mind, and Lord Murray knew he had saved her for the last because she was his preference. She was not too young, she had common sense, superior understanding and a good nature. The red hair that Englishmen evidently disliked he found quite beautiful, and her candid hazel eyes held infinite appeal. However, he had no idea if she liked him. She did not flirt with him as Miss Laurence did, and the generous friendliness with which she treated him was the same she bestowed upon everyone. According to Miss Atwood, Miss Hartwell had been out for several years. He could not believe she had received no offers in that time. Perhaps she was one of those rare women who chose to remain in the single state.

Lord Murray pictured each of the three women in his castle and came to a decision. Miss Hartwell. No one else fit quite perfectly. Lady Sheridan was too cool and remote, Miss Laurence too flighty and immature. The only way he would find out if Miss Hartwell would consider his proposal was to ask her. He would be attending a card party that evening with the Atwoods and would endeavour to find a moment to speak with her there.

PHOEBE STARED AT HER CARDS, willing herself to concentrate on her hand, but it was no use. She could not ignore Wilfred, who had been making urgent signs to her from the doorway on and off for the past hour. She very much feared she was letting her partner down, and was glad she happened to be as good-natured a lady as Mrs. Phelps.

Finally, the hand of whist was over, and she excused herself from the game. She made her way to the refreshment room, feeling sure Wilfred would see her leave and join her there. Her supposition proved to be correct, for she had barely obtained a glass of lemonade when Wilfred was at her side.

"Miss Hartwell, would you speak to me a moment in private?" he asked urgently, running his hand through his hair in a nervous gesture.

Phoebe could tell the impropriety of his request had not even occurred to him. However, he looked so harassed that she did not feel she could in good conscience refuse.

"I think I shall be forced to accede to your request if I wish to be able to acquit myself creditably with the cards this evening," she said lightly.

Wilfred had the grace to look slightly abashed. "I'm sorry, Miss Hartwell. It's just that it *is* important."

"Very well." Phoebe set down her glass of lemonade and followed Wilfred to a small room behind the porter's hall. She seated herself on a rather outdated sofa with crocodile feet and noted with relief that Wilfred was not so lost to propriety as to close the door.

"What is it, Mr. Atwood?" Phoebe encouraged, as Wilfred, now that he had her attention, seemed unable to speak. He scuffed his boot kicking the marble fireplace and did further damage to his appearance by nervously loosening his cravat and worrying the once-sharp points of his collar. Phoebe waited patiently, sure he would tell her what was on his mind once he got up his courage. Her patience was shortly rewarded, for he soon gave a final tug to his cravat, completely untying the unfortunate piece of linen, and turned to face her with a rather sheepish expression.

"Well, Miss Hartwell, it's like this. Tucker and I were having a discussion on the best way to hold one's left hand driving a high perch phaeton. It's obvious the best way is with one's arm extended, elbows straight, but Tucker insists one's left hand should be held at one's knee. Well, the long and short of it is, Miss Hartwell, that Tucker challenged me to a race around the Ring, to prove which is the best way." His recital halted, and Phoebe spoke encouragingly.

"That should not be a problem, Mr. Atwood. I have every faith you will emerge the victor, for I know you are considered an excellent whip."

"If that's all there were to the challenge, Miss Hartwell," Wilfred said, not meeting her eyes. "But you see, we must carry a passenger—much more difficult, y'know, to keep a phaeton steady with two, and," he added in a rush, "the passenger must be female."

"Female? But why?"

"More of a challenge y'know. Must be very careful not to tip and spill her in the road. Problem is," he burst out, "I don't know any females. 'Cept Livvy, and *she* wouldn't help. Would *you* be my passenger, Miss Hartwell?"

Phoebe looked at Mr. Atwood with mingled amusement and surprise. What Wilfred was asking was most improper. Still, she felt she could not refuse his plea. She could not desire Mr. Atwood to be embarrassed before his companions, as he surely would if he failed to race on the terms outlined. And he would no doubt be too embarrassed to ask one of his male friends to find him a female passenger. No gentleman liked to admit he was not a hand with the female sex.

"When is the race to be held, Mr. Atwood?" Phoebe asked. A ridiculous picture of herself seated on a high perch phaeton clutching the seat for dear life while it careened about the Ring in Hyde Park leapt to her mind. What a figure of fun she would appear!

"Saturday morning at six o'clock," he replied, letting out a deep breath as it appeared she was going to agree to his request.

Well, that was early enough that no one would be likely to be about, Phoebe thought philosophically.

Besides, one of the advantages of being only on the fringes of the ton was that one was not well known and people did not pay much attention to one's doings. She would be unlikely to lose her reputation, particularly if she covered her recognizable hair.

"Very well, Mr. Atwood, I shall do as you request, provided that you do not make my identity known to anyone," she stipulated, thinking to preserve her anonymity as far as possible. "But you must never again become involved in a challenge which requires the participation of another whom you have not already asked," she added severely.

Mr. Atwood was too happy at her acquiescence to note Phoebe's mild reprimand.

"I say, you *are* a right'un," he proclaimed, and in his joy took her hands in his and leaned down to place a kiss on her cheek. A faint noise in the hall made Phoebe move her head slightly and Wilfred found that he had missed his mark and placed his lips upon hers. He was surprised at their inviting softness and kissed them lightly. Finding the sensation surprisingly enjoyable, he kept his lips upon hers, tentatively deepening the kiss. Phoebe allowed Wilfred to kiss her a moment, and then gently pushed him away.

"That is enough of that, Mr. Atwood," she said in her best elder-sister voice. She did not wish to hurt his feelings, knowing how easily his ego was bruised, but neither did she wish to encourage him.

"Sorry," Wilfred said, flushing. "I was, um, overcome for a moment. It will not happen again," he announced grandly, feeling quite a man of the world.

LORD MURRAY BACKED SILENTLY away from the door and found his way to the garden, wishing to be alone to think. After coming to the decision to speak to Miss Hartwell that night, he had been pleased to see her at the card party and had watched for an opportunity to talk to her. When he saw her leave her table to go to the refreshment room he had thought that might be his chance, and as soon as he could leave his own table he had gone in search of her.

The last thing he had expected to find was Miss Hartwell and Mr. Atwood in a passionate embrace. He still found it difficult to believe. Perhaps his eyes had been playing tricks upon him. The idea of Miss Hartwell having a fondness for Mr. Atwood would never have occurred to him, although he supposed it should have. Young Atwood, who appeared to be in terror of most females, had always displayed a strong liking for Miss Hartwell. He had, in fact, Lord Murray recalled, said Miss Hartwell was the lady who would be his choice. Lord Murray could not be positive Miss Hartwell returned Atwood's affections, yet he himself remarked she always treated the youth with patience and kindness. She must be five years his elder, Lord Murray mused, but that was not

necessarily a disadvantage. Indeed, perhaps Atwood needed an older, more mature woman.

The devil of it was that he liked Atwood. He was
a callow young gentleman, graceless and bumbling,
but essentially good-hearted. He could not attempt
to cut Atwood out in Miss Hartwell's affections.
Fiercely he submerged the resurgence of his impulse
to throttle that good-natured young man when he
had seen him embracing Miss Hartwell. It had evidently been an intense embrace, for Lord Murray
had noted that Atwood's cravat had been completely undone. Impudent young cub! he thought
angrily. He wondered why, if they returned each
other's affections, they did not announce their betrothal? Probably opposition from Atwood's family,
he guessed. The Atwoods were not likely to approve
their only son's alliance with someone of inferior
rank and, if Miss Atwood's information was to be
believed, no wealth, either.

Lord Murray walked aimlessly about the small
rose garden, trying to come to terms with the new
circumstances. He supposed he was now down to two
choices, Lady Sheridan and Miss Laurence, yet he
felt he could not reconcile himself to the loss of Miss
Hartwell just yet. A picture of Miss Hartwell and
Atwood kissing flashed through his mind again, and
though he knew himself to be the veriest of fools, he
preferred to think that perhaps there was an explanation for the scene he had witnessed. Atwood might
have forced himself on Miss Hartwell, or perhaps the

embrace had been entirely innocent. He would observe Miss Hartwell and Atwood closely when they were in each other's company and see if he could detect mutual affection. After all, marriage was for life and he could not feel comfortable with himself were he to give up too easily.

Now that he had determined a course of action, Lord Murray decided to make his excuses to his hostess and return to the Atwoods' town house. He found he did not want to begin his observations of Miss Hartwell and Atwood together quite yet.

THE NEXT MORNING brought new hope to Lord Murray. Reviewing in broad daylight what he had witnessed the previous evening seemed to confirm his private opinion that it had been quite impossible. He made a good breakfast and went down to the stables to meet Wilfred for their customary morning ride in a cheerful humour. Greeting the callow youth only served to emphasize how ridiculous it was to imagine him in the role of ardent lover.

Lord Murray and Wilfred had become accustomed to their rides being constantly interrupted by those who wished to further their acquaintance with the Scottish lord. Lord Murray was unfailingly polite, but never succumbed to the lures even the most practised of the ladies sent his way. Had he but known it, his aloofness only added to his appeal. He was considered to be the quintessential Highland lord, dour and remote.

Lord Murray was expertly depressing the pretentions of a particularly pushy matron when he heard a gentleman hail Atwood.

"Hope you're in form tomorrow, Atwood. I have a bundle riding on you."

"You won't have cause to regret it," he heard Atwood reply, and the gentleman rode on.

The matron finally proceeded on her way and Lord Murray turned to Atwood with interest.

"Are you engaged to race tomorrow?"

"Yes, Tucker challenged me to a phaeton race. We disagree as to the best method to hold the reins." Remembering his promise to Phoebe, he said nothing about the passengers.

"What method does Tucker endorse?" Lord Murray asked.

"The knee."

"And I observe you prefer holding your elbow straight," he said.

"Yes," Wilfred agreed.

"I prefer your method myself," Lord Murray told him. "I'll have to put some blunt on the outcome. Do you mind if I go along tomorrow and observe the race?" he asked.

"Not at all," Wilfred assured him, flattered to have Lord Murray taking such an interest.

They finished their ride with a frequently interrupted discussion of the finer points of driving, during which Lord Murray almost completely forgot the previous night's worries.

THAT AFTERNOON Lord Murray had his first opportunity to study Miss Hartwell and Mr. Atwood together. Gunther's had announced in the *Gazette* that they had received another cargo of ice from the Greenland Seas and would once again be offering their fruit and cream delicacies. Olivia proposed an outing to the favourite sweets parlour of Society and even suggested Phoebe and Celeste be included, a gesture that earned her an approving look from Lord Murray. He could not know her invitation was motivated by a plan to outshine the two in his presence.

When Lord Murray and the Atwoods collected Phoebe and Celeste, Olivia's spirits rose. Phoebe and Celeste's matching frocks of spotted yellow cambric could not begin to compare to her new pink muslin with its huge puffed sleeves and intricately embroidered skirt. She welcomed the two friends with her sunniest smile.

It was a gay party that drew up to Gunther's in Berkeley Square. They stopped under the shade of one of the many plane trees, and a waiter appeared immediately to take their order.

As they ate their refreshing ices, Lord Murray watched Miss Hartwell and Atwood closely, his observations convincing him there could be no secret understanding between the two. Miss Hartwell hardly looked at Atwood, and Wilfred seemed entirely absorbed in his ice. Of course, it could be that they were being cautious because of the presence of

Miss Atwood, but somehow Lord Murray did not think that was the case.

"Simply delicious," Celeste said, finishing her ice and licking her perfect lips to get every last taste. "I must have another."

"Do you think that would be wise, Miss Laurence?" Olivia commented. "You must think of your complexion."

Celeste ignored Olivia's remark, and Lord Murray summoned a waiter to bring Celeste another ice. While she was waiting for it, a barouche halted beside their carriage and an attractive but haughty-looking woman scanned their party.

"Lord Murray, Mr. Atwood, Miss Atwood, good afternoon," she said, only recognizing the presence of Phoebe and Celeste with a slight nod.

"Lady Jersey, good afternoon," Olivia responded, delighted. This encounter must show Lord Murray that Celeste and Phoebe were not truly accepted in the best society and that he should reconsider his partiality for them. Her idea for the outing had been truly inspired.

"I hope you plan to attend my rout this evening with the Atwoods, Lord Murray?" Lady Jersey enquired. Upon receiving a reply in the affirmative, she instructed her driver to move on.

"Snooty old cat," Celeste muttered.

Phoebe said nothing, but she could tell by Olivia's smug expression that she felt her superiority had been established beyond dispute. She wondered how

Olivia could be so blind. Surely it was obvious that Lord Murray was not so shallow a gentleman as to base his friendships on rank alone. She glanced at him and he smiled at her reassuringly. Phoebe felt her heart give an odd little jump.

Since coming to recognize her growing affection for Lord Murray, Phoebe was experiencing a new kind of excitement and awareness whenever he was present. Also a new kind of pain when she saw other women behave in a coquettish manner towards him. Even to see Celeste so openly trying to gain his attention disturbed her. She considered confiding in Celeste, but fought doing so quite yet. Celeste would likely tease, and her feelings were too new and dear to expose to even the most gentle jest.

Another carriage, this one containing Miss Markham and her mother, stopped next to theirs and Mrs. Markham invited them all, but Lord Murray in particular, to her musicale. Phoebe sighed softly. Lord Murray was so greatly in demand. Did she really have any chance of being the one to win his affections?

CHAPTER FIVE

PHOEBE TUCKED THE last strand of her bright hair out of sight under her bonnet and surveyed herself carefully in the glass. Good. With her hair covered and her deepest brimmed bonnet on, no one should be able to identify her, from a distance, at any rate. Although it was not likely anyone would pay much attention to her anyway, it was just as well not to take unnecessary risks. While she did not feel she was doing anything improper, some might consider her behaviour hoydenish at the least.

Twenty minutes before the hour. If the race were to begin at six, Wilfred had best arrive soon. Phoebe hoped to leave and return with no one the wiser, but if she should be missed she had instructed Sara to say she had gone for a ride in the Park. Which was true, as far as it went.

She heard a clatter upon the street and looked out. Wilfred's phaeton was just pulling up. She slipped quietly out of the house and Wilfred silently assisted Phoebe into his vehicle. As she settled herself upon the seat, Phoebe noticed Celeste waving to her from the window next door and waved back. She was glad to have been able to persuade Celeste not to attend the race.

Wilfred was keyed up and chattered on while Phoebe wondered just how she was going to contrive to stay in her seat once the racing began. She had never been in a high perch phaeton before and was rather alarmed to note that the body sat directly over the front wheels and that she was extremely high off the ground.

When they arrived at the Park, Phoebe did not get down, fearing that if she did she might be reluctant to get back up or that someone might recognize her if they saw her up close. There were several people assembled at the Ring. Mr. Tucker, Wilfred's challenger, had already arrived and the loudly dressed female in his phaeton was laughing immodestly at something he said. Tucker's passenger was not one of the beau monde—that was evident. Phoebe was relieved to notice most of the others appeared to be young sporting gentlemen such as Wilfred—gentlemen unlikely to recognize her. Then she spied Lord Murray, his large form unmistakable. Oh dear, she thought, wondering why she had not considered that he might be present, given the friendship that seemed to have sprung up between him and Wilfred. She could not imagine what he would think if he were to recognize her. She wanted to gain his attention and interest, but not this way!

Phoebe did not have long to worry about Lord Murray, however, for Wilfred sprang back up into the phaeton and he and Tucker lined up in the Ring, the circular drive in Hyde Park. The signal was given, and they were off. Phoebe felt herself tip backwards at the sudden start, and soon forgot all her other worries as her main concern became remaining in the phaeton. The high vehicle dipped and swayed most alarmingly, and Phoebe clutched ignominiously at the edge of the seat. As it continued to dip, surge and sway, Phoebe was thankful that at least she did not have a weak stomach. The wind caught under the deep brim of her bonnet and she bent forward in an effort to keep it from blowing off.

She noticed without caring that Tucker was in the lead. Wilfred did not seem concerned, however, and he slowly gained on his opponent. Phoebe could hear Tucker's passenger's high-pitched shrieks over the thundering of the horses' hooves and the grating of the wheels on the dirt surface. Wilfred flicked his whip lightly, and with another sickening surge, his phaeton drew up even with Tucker's. The huge wheels seemed to come dangerously close to Phoebe's uneducated eyes, and she cravenly closed them. However, the feeling of rushing blindly down a tunnel was not much better, and she opened them again, just as a loud shout went up from the spectators. She saw with relief that they were nearing the end of the course, and prayed that she would stay in her seat until the race was over. She could hear Tucker's phaeton close behind, but he did not pass them, and Wilfred crossed the finish line a whole length ahead.

Wilfred, overjoyed with his victory, gave a shout and jumped down, to be surrounded by gentlemen who pounded him heartily on his back. A groom rushed forward to care for the horses, but no one thought to help Phoebe. Phoebe, anxious to feel the earth beneath her feet once more, looked down to see if she dared jump. She carefully swung her legs over the edge of the seat and let go. However, she had misjudged the height, and when she hit the ground the force of her fall pitched her forward into the dirt.

Wilfred was immediately at Phoebe's side, assisting her up and apologizing profusely.

"You are not injured, I hope, Miss Hartwell? Forgive me," he begged, concern evident in his voice.

Phoebe brushed herself off shakily. "Only my pride," she said trying to laugh. "I cannot think how I came to be so clumsy."

Reassured as to her safety, Wilfred remembered his triumph and hugged her enthusiastically. "We won!" he cried, emboldened to give her a victory kiss.

LORD MURRAY WATCHED Wilfred embrace Phoebe with a sinking heart. When he had first seen the woman in Wilfred's phaeton, he had not been able to believe his eyes. Indeed, he had thought perhaps he was mistaken as to her identity, for her face was difficult to see under the deep-brimmed bonnet. But when she had turned towards the sun, there was no denying that the lady was Miss Hartwell.

His first reaction had been anger that Atwood intended to expose Miss Hartwell to the dangers of a race. How could Atwood do such a foolhardy thing if he loved her? Lord Murray had considered intervening, but hesitated, knowing he had no real right to do so. He had watched the race with a great deal more concern about the safety of Miss Hartwell than the safety of the money he had placed upon the outcome, and felt relief beyond compare when it was over.

When he saw that Miss Hartwell had been left in the phaeton he had started forward to assist her down, but before he could get there she had jumped. Though he had rushed towards her, greatly alarmed by her fall, Wilfred had reached her side first. Lord Murray observed Atwood's solicitous manner and fervent embrace with combined anger and despair. Even he must acknowledge there was affection between the two. Miss Hartwell must care for Atwood deeply to have participated in the race, exposing herself to danger and censure. He had no choice but to accept the obvious. Biting his lip, he strode forward to congratulate Atwood.

THAT AFTERNOON Lord Murray sought solitude in the Atwoods' library. It was the most restful room in the house with its book-lined walls and comfortable armchairs, and was rarely used by anyone but the baron. It was early, but Lord Murray helped himself to the decanter of port Lord Atwood kept in the room. He sank into one of the armchairs and prepared to think.

With Miss Hartwell out of the running, only two of his original four possible brides remained—Miss Laurence and Lady Sheridan. He had best make a decision between the two and get it over with. He did not wish to begin his search anew. There was no time and he hadn't the heart. But before he could begin to consider the matter in earnest a footstep sounded outside the door and his host entered.

"Do you mind if I join you?" Lord Atwood asked. "If I am not disturbing you, that is."

"Not at all," Lord Murray said politely.

Lord Atwood poured himself some port and settled into a comfortable armchair across from Lord Murray's.

"Have you come to a decision in your search for a wife yet?" Lord Atwood enquired of his guest after some polite conversation.

Lord Murray smiled ruefully. "No. I am beginning to think I was inexcusably arrogant or incredibly paper-skulled to think I could come and select a bride out-of-hand."

"You could." Lord Atwood smiled. "You are the envy of all us plain Englishmen. There is not an eligible woman in Society who would not be willing to toss her bonnet over the windmill for the handsome Highland lord."

"Perhaps it might so appear, but it is not quite so simple," Lord Murray said seriously. "My bride will be chatelaine of a remote Scottish castle. We have neither all the comforts you English are accustomed to, nor the diversions. While life in the Highlands may be romantic in a poem, the reality is very different."

"Is there no one you have more of an interest in than the others? Perhaps I could give you information on her background or personality that would help you make a better-informed choice," the baron offered helpfully.

Lord Murray hesitated, taking a sip of his port to disguise his discomfort.

His host smiled understandingly. "Do not hesitate to be honest. I will not say I did not hope at first that you might take a liking to Olivia, but I soon came to see it would not do. Olivia needs a husband who will control her. You would expect your wife to control herself."

"I had rather thought of Lady Sheridan or Miss Laurence," Lord Murray confided, naming the two remaining of his original four.

Lord Atwood looked thoughtful. "Lady Sheridan and Miss Laurence. Both good choices. Of course, Mr. Laurence works in the City, but nonetheless Miss Laurence is the granddaughter of an earl."

Lord Murray raised his eyebrows in surprise.

"Oh, yes," Lord Atwood continued, noting his reaction. "Mrs. Laurence is Lord March's daughter. He disapproved of her match with Laurence and cut her off completely. He has never communicated with her since the marriage, I believe. Still, Miss Laurence is of good blood, and I believe Mr. Laurence is quite well-to-pass.

"Now, Lady Sheridan. She would also be a good choice. Her beauty and breeding are self-evident. If she would accept an offer, that is. She has been wearing the willow these past nine years. Her betrothed was killed in the fighting in Egypt. She must be near eight-and-twenty now. Her parents despair of her ever marrying, and I'm sure they would be glad if you made an offer."

Lord Murray was taken aback at this information. Lady Sheridan did not look to be eight-and-twenty. He did not consider her age to be an insurmountable problem, but he was not sure he wished to marry someone wearing the willow. One would always feel one were a poor substitute. A living rival he could compete with, but not one enshrined in a lady's memory. Not, he thought wryly, that he should dismiss Lady Sheridan out of hand for that reason. Would not any woman he married be his second choice? Still, of the two he felt he preferred Miss Laurence.

"If only Miss Laurence were not so young," he said aloud.

"If I might make a suggestion," the baron offered, "why not make a conditional offer? Don't make it official yet, but invite Miss Laurence to travel to the Highlands and stay with you this summer. See how she likes it. If you find you don't suit, no one need be any the wiser. An excursion to the Highlands, as I understand it, is all the rage anyhow," he finished wryly, thinking of his own daughter's insistence on a visit to Lake Katrine in July.

"Thank you, sir, that is an excellent idea," Lord Murray agreed, feeling somewhat heartened to now have his course decided, but he could not deny that he was also somewhat disheartened that the outcome had not been resolved as he would have preferred.

ONCE LORD MURRAY had made his decision to offer for Miss Laurence, he felt there was no point in further delay. He called upon Mr. Laurence the very next evening. He had never met Celeste's father before, since Mr. Laurence spent his days in the City and chose not to attend evening entertainments with his wife and daughter. Lord Murray found himself favourably impressed. In appearance, Mr. Laurence was tall and thin, with greying hair and penetrating eyes. The two men exchanged greetings and smiled, each satisfied with what he saw in the other.

"Please sit down, Lord Murray. May I offer you refreshment?" Mr. Laurence asked courteously, seating himself after his guest.

"No, thank you, Mr. Laurence. I shall come straight to the point. I should like your permission to make your daughter an offer of marriage."

"Celeste?" Mr. Laurence enquired needlessly. "Forgive me, she is my only daughter and of course you must be speaking of her, yet I am surprised. She is very young, and not, if I may be frank, the wife I would expect a man in your lordship's position to choose."

"It is true Miss Laurence is very young," Lord Murray agreed, "but she has a warm heart, a quick mind, and of course she is very beautiful. However, owing to her tender years, I would like to suggest that the betrothal be unofficial at first. I propose that Miss Laurence and her mother, of course, come to Scotland and stay as my guests at Castle Abermaise so that Miss Laurence may see if she likes living in the Highlands. If she does not, she can return to London having simply been on an excursion to the Highlands such as many are planning this summer."

Mr. Laurence nodded his approval. "That is an excellent notion. However, I doubt it will serve, for my wife is not in robust health. She suffered a severe bout of influenza earlier this year, and I doubt she is up to a long journey."

"Could Miss Laurence's friend Miss Hartwell accompany her?" Lord Murray suggested impulsively. "I assure you there would be no impropriety in their staying at the castle, for my aunt is in residence there, as are several other of my kinsmen."

As soon as Lord Murray spoke the words he wished he had not. How could he have Miss Hartwell staying in the castle as well, given his feelings for her? He had no business inviting the woman he most desired to share his castle with the woman he planned to make his wife. However, it was too late to retract his suggestion, and Mr. Laurence heartily approved the plan.

"Yes, that would be acceptable. Miss Hartwell has a good head upon her shoulders, and I would not worry about Celeste if she were in her charge. If Miss Hartwell will agree to accompany Celeste, I shall give my permission." He laughed. "Here we are making plans and you do not know if Celeste is even of a mind to accept your suit. It is up to her, of course. I shall not attempt to persuade her to anything against her will."

Mr. Laurence rang the bell and instructed a footman to summon Celeste.

In a few moments, Celeste, clad in a simple white gown in the classical style, arrived at the study door. She gave Lord Murray a quick look and addressed her father.

"You sent for me, Papa?"

"Lord Murray has something he wishes to say to you," Mr. Laurence explained, as he rose from his desk. "You may speak to him in private. Your mama and I shall join you shortly," he said, leaving the two together.

Now that the moment was upon him, Lord Murray felt strangely uncomfortable. Celeste waited patiently for him to speak, her eyes downcast, hands clasped demurely before her, obviously aware of what was to come. He forced himself to speak, knowing that once he did he would be irrevocably committed.

"Miss Laurence, in the days I have been in London I have seen much to admire in you. I think my purpose in coming to London is not unknown—and I have sometimes thought you were not indifferent to me. I should like you to travel to my castle in Scotland this summer, and if you find it congenial, I should like you to stay."

Miss Laurence looked up at him with an air of mingled excitement and triumph.

"Do I understand correctly you are making me an offer, Lord Murray?" she asked, an impish expression on her piquant face.

"Yes," Lord Murray said, amused at his inept proposal of marriage.

"Then I thank you, Lord Murray, and I should like very much to accompany you to Scotland this summer."

Her words reminded Lord Murray of the one condition Mr. Laurence had placed upon his consent.

"Your father agrees to these plans only if your friend Miss Hartwell will be able to accompany you, since your mother is not well enough for such a long journey."

Lord Murray was surprised to see that these words seemed to evince more excitement than his actual offer.

"Oh, that will be wonderful, Lord Murray!" she exclaimed, clapping her hands together. "I am sure Phoebe will agree to go."

Lord Murray looked at Miss Laurence uncertainly. He supposed he should kiss her; that was what one did when one made an offer. However, he felt surprisingly little desire to do so, despite her undeniable beauty and youthful charm. He took her hand, noting absently that it was an exceptionally soft and well-formed one, and brought it to his lips. Miss Laurence seemed to find this a satisfactory seal to their betrothal, and when they were joined soon after by Mr. and Mrs. Laurence, the couple wisely refrained from commenting on the decorous behaviour of the newly engaged pair.

PHOEBE WAS PREPARING to retire that evening when Celeste burst into her bedchamber.

"You will never think what has happened, Phoebe!" her friend exclaimed. "Lord Murray has offered for me."

"What?" Phoebe cried, turning to face Celeste with a cold sinking feeling in her stomach. Lord Murray had offered for Celeste? Somehow she had not expected him to do so. She knew he enjoyed

Celeste's company, but she had thought he looked upon her more as an impish younger sister than a possible bride.

"Yes, he has truly offered," Celeste confirmed excitedly. "He is with Papa now, working out the details of the settlements."

She stood before Phoebe and took her hands in her own. "We have won!" she exclaimed, squeezing her friend's hands tightly. "But it is to be unofficial for now, which is a pity, for I cannot tell Olivia. Never mind, she will be jealous as Juno when she hears I am gone to stay at Abermaise this summer. For that is what I am to do—Lord Murray wishes me to find if Scotland is congenial to me before anything is announced. As if it could be otherwise! And best of all, you are to accompany me!"

Phoebe pulled abruptly away from Celeste, busying herself with lighting another candle so that she could regain control over her emotions. Celeste to marry Lord Murray. She could barely fathom that such a thing could happen or that she was not simply having a bad dream from which she would awaken. But for her to accompany Celeste to Lord Murray's castle and be forced to observe his courting of her? No! She could not possibly. Not when she was in love with Lord Murray. For the first time she had now admitted to herself the depth of her feelings for Lord Murray, and the pain of knowing she was to lose him was more than she could bear. Never having any cause to envy her friend before, Phoebe knew she would give anything to exchange places with her.

"I do not think I could possibly accompany you, Celeste," she said, trying to keep her voice steady and not betray the turbulent emotions she was experiencing. "My sister—not to mention the expense—"

"But you *must*," Celeste interrupted, recapturing Phoebe's hands and looking at her pleadingly, not understanding why her friend was not as excited as she. "I cannot possibly go alone. Besides, this is what we dreamed of, what we planned for, going to the Highlands together. You will find a Scottish lord there, too, and we shall live next to each other happily ever after," she proclaimed, using the favourite line of nurses to end the stories they told their charges. "As for the expense, Papa will stand it. He told me he insisted."

Phoebe found she could not ignore her friend's plea, however she wished she might. Celeste had been her closest friend for nearly fifteen years. She was truly like her own sister. It was not Celeste's fault Phoebe had been so foolish as to give her heart where it was not returned. How could she be so selfish as to sacrifice Celeste's happiness to her disappointment that she had not been Lord Murray's choice?

"If Mama and Papa give their consent, I shall go," Phoebe agreed at last, ruthlessly quashing her misgivings.

CHAPTER SIX

PHOEBE AND CELESTE stood side by side contemplating the view before them while the coachman, groom and postilions waited with the carriage.

"It is precisely like the scenery described in *Lady of the Lake*," Celeste said breathlessly as she looked over the Perthshire countryside spread beneath them.

> "So wondrous wild, the whole might seem
> The scenery of a fairy dream,'"

Phoebe quoted. For once, she thought, she was not amused by Celeste's romantical outpourings, but in full agreement with them. The Highlands of Scotland were fully as rugged, majestic and sublimely beautiful as the pictures Mr. Scott had so vividly painted in his poem. Purple mountains rose precipitously in the distance, flanked by gentle hills covered with oak and beech. A large lake filled the floor of the valley below, its placid surface shining brightly in the afternoon sun, flanked by meadows and fields dotted with farmhouses. At the far end of the lake Phoebe could see a large stone castle.

"That must be Castle Abermaise," Phoebe said, pointing.

Celeste looked in the direction Phoebe indicated, and at the sight of the impressive edifice, felt the doubts that had occasionally assailed her during the long journey vanish.

For several minutes the two friends gazed wordlessly. Then a strong breeze ruffled the lake's surface and blew their skirts about, bringing Phoebe back to the present.

"We had best continue, Celeste, or Lord Murray will think we have had an accident," she said, walking back to the carriage. With a final sigh, Celeste followed her, and they joined their maids in the carriage for the last stage of their journey.

Lord Murray had travelled by horseback with them for most of their trip to Scotland, arranging the accommodations at inns and seeing to their comfort. That morning, however, he had ridden ahead to see that all was satisfactorily prepared for their reception at the castle.

Phoebe awaited the end of their travels with some trepidation. She had not yet decided whether she had made the right decision to accompany Celeste to Perthshire. She had tried to overcome her feelings for Lord Murray, and had hoped that during the long journey he might reveal some less admirable qualities that would make her task easier. But his thoughtfulness and care for their comfort had only increased her admiration. Moreover, his demeanor towards Celeste had made it somewhat easier for her to forget his betrothal, for he had treated her not like a lover but like a sister. Celeste, who had seemed to view the journey as an adventure, apparently saw nothing amiss in Lord Murray's behaviour towards her. To be sure, Phoebe did not really know how Celeste truly felt where Lord Murray was concerned. She had done her best to avoid the subject, fearing she might inadvertently give away her own feelings.

The castle they had seen in the distance grew slowly larger, and Celeste's eyes began to sparkle in anticipation.

"Oh, Phoebe, I never did really think my dream of going to the Highlands would come true," she confessed, "but it has. Did you ever imagine things could be so wonderful?"

Phoebe smiled and pretended to be absorbed in the view outside, but her heart was beginning to beat strongly with emotion. Within minutes she would enter the castle she had dared to dream she might be mistress of—but as a guest instead.

The carriage rolled to a stop, and Lord Murray strode forward to personally assist Phoebe and Celeste down.

"Welcome to Castle Abermaise, Miss Hartwell, Miss Laurence," he said formally, with unmistakable pride in his voice.

For a moment Phoebe was awed, and she stood gazing at the castle in wonder. She and Celeste had never been out of London before, and while Buckingham Palace and Carlton House were very fine, somehow neither had the impact this great old stone castle had in its lonely and forbidding splendour next to the great lake. Grey stone turrets rose forbiddingly into the sky, and the face of the castle presented an impassive front broken only by the few narrow arched windows.

Her reverie was interrupted by Celeste, who pulled her impatiently by the arm. Phoebe saw Lord Murray was waiting to usher them into the castle, and she followed after her friend. Phoebe's first impression of the castle interior was one of spaciousness. There was an immensely high ceiling, and she soon realized that the huge room they had entered occupied the entire floor, or very nearly so. Faint light entered through the deep-set narrow windows, which had seats built beneath them into the thick walls. A few plain chairs were scattered about the stone-paved floor, two large fireplaces were on opposite walls, and she noticed a winding stairway at the far end of the room. At the head of the hall a great chair and some benches were fixed to the wall, a table of boards on trestles before them. Celeste, standing still beside Phoebe, was unusually quiet, and Phoebe sensed she was dismayed at the starkness of the great hall.

Before she could take in all the details, Phoebe's attention was diverted by two people advancing towards them—a plump comfortable-looking woman with thick grey hair partially covered by a kerchief, and a tall forbidding-looking man with thinning hair. Without waiting to be presented, the woman launched into speech.

"Sic bonnie lassies! But whaur's your havins? They'll be sair forjeskit and drouthy, I've na doot."

Celeste looked at Phoebe in bewilderment, unable to understand the woman's broad Lowland Scots dialect. The tall man saw Celeste's confusion and came to her aid.

"How could you expect the lassie to understand such blather?" he asked the woman, and then turned to Celeste. "Mrs. Baird asks where our manners are, for you must be tired and thirsty," he translated for Celeste in perfectly understandable English, albeit with a different lilting cadence.

Celeste's face cleared "Yes, something to drink would be delightful."

After a disdainful look at Celeste's translator, the matronly woman bustled away, and the man led them to the board table. They had no sooner seated themselves than the woman returned, bearing tea and two plates of what appeared to be a kind of porridge.

"If you are wondering what the porridge is, it is called oatmeal brose," Lord Murray told his guests. "You will find we Scots eat many dishes made from oats." He noticed Celeste's enquiring look at the woman.

"Mrs. Baird is my housekeeper, and this is Balneaves, my butler," Lord Murray explained, indicating the tall man, who was placing a cup of a strong-smelling drink before his master. "In the Highlands it is customary to take care of the immediate needs of one's guests before introductions."

A practical idea, Phoebe thought, as she tried the porridge, which tasted surprisingly good. As she ate, Phoebe glanced about the room, seeing things she had missed on first inspection. She noticed there were various other people in the hall and was puzzled by some piles of what appeared to be brush along one wall. A sweet pungent odour seemed to permeate the room.

When Phoebe and Celeste had finished their tea and brose, Lord Murray made the suggestion that perhaps they would like to retire to their chamber after such a fatiguing journey. Both women assured him that they were not overtired and did not need to rest just yet, so Lord Murray introduced them to the other occupants of the room. Phoebe was amazed to learn that they all seemed to be relatives, for Lord Murray referred to them as cousins. There were several Murrays, a Spalding and two Dunbars. They were all men—large, roughly dressed and with odd-looking footwear. Their expressions were friendly and hospitable despite their rather fierce appearance.

One in particular stood out to Phoebe, the only one clad in full Highland dress. He was a short man, or perhaps he only seemed to be short in the room of giants, Phoebe thought. He had hair as red as her own, a wild-looking beard and piercing hazel eyes. He was presented as Dinsmore, the piper. Phoebe instinctively curtsied to the proud-looking man, her action earning her a look of approval from Lord Murray.

"Now we shall go upstairs to present you to my aunt," Lord Murray said when all those in the hall had been introduced. "She regrets her infirmities prevented her from coming down to greet you."

Phoebe and Celeste followed Lord Murray up the spiral stairs and into a dark hallway faintly illumined by the deep set windows. They came to a door which he opened, and they stepped into another world. The room was wainscotted and a rich Brussels carpet of predominantly cream and blue covered the floor. A fire burned cheerfully in a carved white marble fireplace and fine Chippendale furniture was artfully arranged to afford comfort as well as beauty.

Lord Murray spoke, addressing the look of relief he had seen in his betrothed's eyes.

"My grandfather partitioned this floor into smaller rooms and my mother furnished them to her taste. This is the floor where my aunt and I have our chambers; my kinsmen stay below, and the servants are on the second floor."

He led them through into a second drawing room where a frail-looking lady with snow-white hair sat regally upon an open armchair covered with petit-point.

"Aunt Margaret, may I present Miss Hartwell and Miss Laurence to you. Miss Hartwell, Miss Laurence, my aunt, Lady Melville."

Phoebe and Celeste curtsied gracefully.

"I am pleased to meet you," Lady Melville said sincerely. "I trust you are not overfatigued from your journey and have been given refreshment?"

Phoebe assured her of their care, and Lady Melville bade them be seated.

"Who were all the people below?" Celeste asked, unable to restrain her curiosity. "I did not realize you had so many relatives who lived with you, Lord Murray."

"You will find things rather different here than they are in England, Miss Laurence," Lord Murray replied. "While I call them my cousins, kinsmen or even foster-kin might be a more accurate term. Some are so distantly related that the connexion is difficult to trace. However, their families have been associated with the Murrays for many years. They provide labour, and in return I provide them with food and shelter."

"They live below stairs?" Phoebe commented, remembering his earlier remark, and wondering where they could possibly stay, for she had seen only the one large room.

"They wrap themselves in their plaids and sleep on piles of heather," he said, and watched their faces for their reactions. This was their first exposure to one of the harsher realities of life in the relatively poor Highlands, and he wondered what their response would be.

That explained the brush piles and pungent smell, Phoebe thought, but Celeste looked shocked at the idea of so housing one's relatives, however distantly connected. Lady Melville saw Celeste's distress and tried to explain.

"If we should offer our kinsmen rooms on this floor with us, provided we had that many, they would not accept, but rather be offended, viewing it as charity. What they are given is what they have a right to, as members of our 'clan.' Those kinsmen with families are given small cottages, and the single men reside in the castle." She smiled kindly at Celeste. "We Scots have very strong ideas of independence. You will become accustomed to our ways with time, and not think them so odd," she promised.

"Perhaps I should warn you we take dinner with all kinsmen in the great hall below," Lord Murray commented. "However, breakfast and supper will be served up here."

Celeste looked rather dazed, and Phoebe took the opportunity to ask a question that had been teasing her.

"Is Mrs. Baird from another district?" she enquired, thinking of the housekeeper's thick accent, so different from the lilting one of the other kinsmen and servants.

"Yes. My mother brought Mrs. Baird here when she came to Castle Abermaise as a bride," Lord Murray said. "My mother was a Lowlander. Lowlanders speak a stronger dialect than Highlanders, although you will sometimes hear Highlanders speak Gaelic, which you will not understand at all.

"You may have noticed that Balneaves and Mrs. Baird do not appear to get along," Lord Murray continued with a smile. "Should you hear them arguing, do not let it trouble you. Their feud is of longstanding, and mostly for show. The Highlanders preyed upon the Lowlanders for generations, and some resentment is still felt."

"Like in *Lady of the Lake*," Celeste commented. "The Highlanders in the poem called the Lowlanders 'Saxons.'"

The sparkle reappeared in Celeste's eyes. With the resilience of youth she had bounced back from her initial disappointment and was covering the whole with romanticism.

Phoebe and Lord Murray exchanged a look that suggested they were in agreement that Celeste had much to learn, and then Phoebe averted her eyes. Such wordless communication shared with Lord Murray was not wise. Under the circumstances encouraging even a silent bond could only lead to pain.

"I think it is time Miss Laurence and Miss Hartwell were shown their rooms," Lady Melville proclaimed, ringing for a maid. "They will wish to rest before supper."

Phoebe and Celeste had been given adjoining chambers with a connecting door. Phoebe's room was tastefully decorated in gold and grey, and Celeste's in shades of rose. Both had the Chippendale furniture Lord Murray's mother had evidently admired.

"I am glad the rooms on this floor have been re-done," Celeste confessed to her friend. "The Great Hall is so dreary."

"Yes, but I liked it," Phoebe said. "It spoke to me of history."

"You are welcome to it. I prefer modern times," Celeste said, and sank onto a graceful bench at the foot of Phoebe's bed. "I am beginning to feel tired. Perhaps we could have our suppers on trays in here tonight."

"That is a good idea. I shall ask," Phoebe agreed. It had been a very tiring journey, and now they had arrived, she was beginning to succumb to fatigue. Phoebe felt she could sleep for two days, at least.

WHEN PHOEBE AWOKE the next morning she lay a moment in that confused state sometimes caused by waking in a new place. There was an odd noise, too, impinging on her consciousness. The din grew louder and she came fully awake, recognizing the sound as bagpipes and remembering that she was now in Scotland. She glanced at the small ormolu clock—it was early, barely nine of the clock.

A tap sounded at their connecting door, and Celeste came in, clad in a dressing gown.

"Whatever do they mean, making such a noise so early in the morning?" she complained, covering her ears.

"I believe it is bagpipes."

"Yes, of course, it is bagpipes," Celeste said impatiently, "but where is it coming from?"

Phoebe was also curious about the source of the early morning music. She pulled on a dressing gown and slid her feet into some slippers, and the two ventured out of the room into the hallway.

"I think it is coming up the stairs," Phoebe said as they paused a moment outside the door.

Seeing no one about, they made their way to the stairway and peeped over the railing into the Great Hall below. The sight that met their eyes was both diverting and impressive. The piper, Dinsmore, in full Highland dress, was striding back and forth across the hall, playing his pipes. Brightly coloured ribands tied to his chanters flowed down to trail along the floor, and various of the kinsmen followed in his wake, seemingly entranced by the sound of the pipes. Phoebe watched intently, fascinated by the manner in which Dinsmore manipulated the bag with his arm and coaxed such beautiful music from the instrument. She found the stirring music appealed to something deep inside her.

Celeste, however, was not so enchanted. "Why ever is he playing so early," she complained again. "How is one expected to be able to sleep?"

Phoebe was about to reply when she heard someone approaching, and she and Celeste turned around to find Lord Murray had joined them. Phoebe flushed, feeling embarrassed to be caught like a child peeping over the bannister, but Celeste was not so easily put out of countenance when she was irritated by something.

"We were wakened by the noise and wondered where it could be coming from," she explained. "Must he play the pipes so early?"

"Nine o'clock is not considered early here, Miss Laurence," Lord Murray replied, finding the sight of the two girls in their dishabille quite captivating. Evidently, they had escaped their rooms before their maids saw them, for their hair was loose, and their hastily donned dressing gowns revealed their night-rails underneath. "Dinsmore plays every morning," he added, trying to focus his eyes strictly on their faces.

"Every morning?" Celeste repeated, aghast. "Can he not do so later? We are not accustomed to rising so early. In London during the Season one often sleeps until noon."

"I can ask him, Miss Laurence, but I cannot promise he will agree."

"Why don't you simply order him to?" Celeste asked, perplexed.

"It is not quite that simple. Being a piper is a hereditary office in the families of Highlanders. Dinsmore has the *right* to play the pipes in the morning. I cannot forbid it. It is not within my power."

Celeste rolled her eyes at Phoebe as if to say the customs here were beyond belief. Phoebe smiled, and found herself exchanging another look of understanding with Lord Murray.

"I promise to speak to him and shall do my best for you, Miss Laurence," Lord Murray agreed, thinking how he could not bring himself to call Celeste by her given name despite the fact that their betrothal gave him that right. His eyes kept straying to Phoebe, and he made a strong effort to bring his errant thoughts into line. "I shall see you both in the breakfast room shortly," he said, and left.

"Can you imagine not being able to order a servant to do something," Celeste asked Phoebe as they walked back to their rooms.

"I do not think Dinsmore is considered a servant, precisely," Phoebe responded. "Things *are* very different here, though. I expect we shall become accustomed in time, as Lady Melville said."

"Perhaps," Celeste said, but silently she rather doubted she would ever become accustomed to the pipes and hoped Lord Murray would be able to persuade Dinsmore not to play them.

THE SIDEBOARDS in the breakfast room were heavily laden with boiled eggs, cream, butter, brose, bannock, goat cheese, venison pastry, ham and wheat bread. Phoebe suspected the ham and wheat bread had been included particularly for the English guests. She helped herself to a plate of oatmeal brose, remembering it from the previous afternoon.

"You like our solid Scots fare?" Lord Murray enquired, noting Phoebe's choice. "I told you you were a Scots lassie."

"Yes, I find I quite like oats," Phoebe confessed. "I must take after my Scottish grandmother."

"I do not care for oats," Celeste said candidly. "I prefer toast and preserves."

"I do myself," Lady Melville said kindly, not wishing her nephew's fiancée to feel she must like everything Scottish.

Lord Murray smiled at Celeste's frankness. This was going to be interesting. He suspected there would be many aspects of Scottish life his betrothed would not find to her liking. Being an only child, she would be used to having things as she wished, and since her father was fairly wealthy, she would not be accustomed to deprivations or having to make do. He wondered how his kinsmen would take to her should she decide to stay and marry him. There were already indications they would not be willing to make many allowances. When he had spoken to Dinsmore, the piper had refused to stop his morning playing. For a regular guest, he would have ceased to play at all until the guest left, for Highlanders had a very strict code of hospitality. Evidently he felt that since Miss Laurence was to become the lady of the castle she could not be considered an ordinary guest and the sooner she adjusted to their customs, the better.

After breakfast Lord Murray excused himself, saying there were estate matters he had to attend to, and suggested that Phoebe and Celeste might care to walk about his lands.

"Do not be alarmed if one of my kinsmen or servants follows you," he warned. "It is the custom here that the laird and his family and guests never be left alone. The area can be dangerous to those who are not familiar with it."

Phoebe and Celeste decided the idea of a walk was appealing, and after changing into sturdy shoes, they ventured downstairs and into the open air.

Celeste's temper had been on the sour side since being awakened by pipes, but once she was outside her irritations were banished by the beauty of the land. They walked slowly down a footpath that led from the castle to the lake, followed, as Lord Murray had warned, by one of his personal servants, or gillies, as Phoebe had heard them called.

They came to a small rise and stopped, looking out over the lake. Celeste became lost in an airdream, and Phoebe knew she was imagining herself to be Ellen Douglas, the heroine of *Lady of the Lake*, again. She wondered if her young friend would ever learn to reconcile her two Scotlands—the one of her dreams and the one of reality. She feared she would not.

THAT DAY they took their first dinner in the Great Hall with all the kinsmen. Phoebe could tell that the meal was taking the glow off Celeste's newly polished romantic view of the Highlands. They all sat together at the huge board-and-trestle table, Lord Murray in an outsized chair at the head. A gillie stood directly behind him, anticipating his master's every need. But Phoebe was surprised at the lack of deference the others showed their laird. She realized they meant no disrespect as it became clear that his kinsmen all seemed to feel that their opinions were of value as well, and they did not hesitate to voice them, or to disagree with their laird. It made for a noisy, rather boisterous meal.

Lord Murray watched his two guests closely during their first meal in the Hall. He observed that Miss Hartwell was intrigued, while Miss Laurence was uncomfortable. He felt a surge of tender indulgence towards Miss Laurence, recognizing at the same time it was not a feeling generally associated with one's beloved, but rather the natural impulse he as an older experienced person had to protect the young.

Indulgence did not enter into his feelings towards Miss Hartwell. He admired her, for he sensed that she truly liked and appreciated Scottish customs and understood them as Miss Laurence could not. He

could easily imagine himself and Miss Hartwell
sharing an equal fondness for his homeland and for
one another. But such thoughts were dangerous. He
had to keep reminding himself that Miss Hartwell
was already spoken for by Atwood, and that he
himself had spoken for Miss Laurence. He turned to
his betrothed with an encouraging smile and engaged her in conversation, trying to make her feel
less strange.

CELESTE WAS GLAD to escape back upstairs after
dinner to the familiarity and security of the more
comfortable rooms. As her maid, Alice, helped her
dress to go riding with Phoebe, she reflected that not
quite everything here at Castle Abermaise was as she
had dreamed it would be. The customs were strange,
although the scenery was everything she had imagined. She wondered if the walk in the moonlight with
her Scottish lord in full Highland dress would ever
materialize.

What an odd sensation that she had to keep reminding herself she was in fact betrothed to Lord
Murray. She did not *feel* betrothed. Her feelings for
Lord Murray were not at all clear to her. Admiration, certainly—one had to admire so well-looking a
gentleman. And respect coupled with a certain
amount of awe, but nothing of the romantic feeling
the novels she had borrowed from the circulating library in London identified as love. In her first excitement over the betrothal, she had not noticed this

distressing lack of emotion, and when she had, had simply told herself that love would develop with time. No doubt this would be the case, she thought optimistically, once they were actually married.

Alice finished arranging Celeste's curls and carefully fastened her mistress' jaunty riding hat on top of her creation. Phoebe tapped at the door, asking if she were ready, and Celeste, feeling happy again, went cheerfully out, certain that all would be well in the end.

CHAPTER SEVEN

"PERHAPS THIS MORNING you might find the time to go over the household accounts with me, Miss Laurence," Lady Melville suggested to Celeste, a hint of censure in her voice.

Phoebe smiled to herself, wondering what pretext Celeste would offer this time. Although everyone in the castle had been advised that the betrothal between Lord Murray and Celeste was not yet official, no one seemed to doubt the eventual outcome. Lady Melville appeared to feel that Celeste should begin learning some of the duties that fell to the lady of a castle, but so far she had had scant success. Celeste always had a plausible reason she could not comply with Lady Melville's wishes. This morning, however, she had evidently run out of excuses.

"If you wish, Lady Melville," Celeste replied with a marked lack of enthusiasm. She looked hopefully at the drawing-room door, as though wishing Lord Murray might come and save her, an unlikely event since he spent most of his mornings dealing with his estate business.

Phoebe's momentary feeling of amusement vanished, to be replaced by one of disquiet. It was becoming more evident to her each day that Celeste would never be happy in Perthshire, although Celeste herself steadfastly refused to consider this possibility. Phoebe supposed Celeste had envisaged herself a romantic heroine in the style of Ellen Douglas too long to easily relinquish the role.

Lady Melville rose and walked slowly to the door with the aid of her cane. Celeste followed reluctantly, bestowing on Phoebe a silent plea to accompany her. Phoebe shook her head and gave her an encouraging smile. The opportunity for a few minutes alone was rare, and she wanted to take advantage of the time to think over their circumstances.

They had been in residence at Castle Abermaise a sennight now, and while it was apparent Celeste was entranced with the beauty of the setting, it was equally obvious she was not comfortable with either the customs or the characters. Neither behaved according to her script. The servants and distant relatives refused to stay in the background as they would in England, and insisted on playing a major part in the lives of the lord and his intended lady. Celeste endured the dinners at the large table downstairs, but one could see she much preferred the suppers upstairs in the relative privacy of the Chippendale rooms. Nor had Celeste developed a liking for the pipes, which amounted to something akin to heresy to the Highlanders.

Thinking of the pipes caused Phoebe to recall the previous Sunday's excursion to church, and she smiled broadly. She and Celeste had prepared to accompany Lord Murray and Lady Melville to services, dressing in simple muslin frocks and thin slippers. Upon going downstairs, they had been surprised to find that instead of riding to church in a carriage, it was the custom for all the kinsmen and servants to walk to worship together with Dinsmore striding ahead playing the pipes. Phoebe had looked at their thin slippers dubiously, but not wishing to make the party late, she did not suggest she and Celeste go back to change their shoes.

That had been a mistake, for long before they had reached the church both were limping badly. Lord Murray's gillie, a large, fierce-looking Highlander, had offered to carry his master's betrothed the rest of the way, an offer which Celeste had found mortifying in the extreme and had refused adamantly. That had not been the end of her trials, however, for when they arrived at the church, Dinsmore had remained outside piping the party in to the "March of Abermaise." Celeste had kept her eyes rigidly fixed on the minister throughout the service, obviously wishing she were anywhere else. She might enjoy being the centre of attention, but she was still young enough to have a horror of being made to appear ridiculous, and evidently that was how she felt. Phoebe knew Celeste hoped that once she was lady of the castle she would be able to consign such customs to the devil, but Phoebe knew better.

Phoebe arose from her chair and went to the window, looking out over the lake. She sighed deeply. She simply could not picture Celeste as lady of Castle Abermaise. She would never fit in. Noticing that the sun was beginning to burn the morning mist away, Phoebe decided to go for a walk. Perhaps that would help raise her depressed spirits.

Donning a sensible hat and her sturdiest shoes, she advised Sara as to where she would be, should Celeste want her later. On her way outside she encountered the piper.

"Good morning, Mr. Dinsmore," she said politely.

"Good morning, Miss Hartwell," he replied. "I see you are going for a walk. Do you mind if I accompany you?"

Phoebe assented cordially. As Lord Murray had warned, she had found it was impossible for either her or Celeste to go anywhere without being accompanied by one of Lord Murray's kinsmen or followed at a respectful distance by one of his gillies. Phoebe felt she would prefer Dinsmore's companionship this morning to that of a silent shadow. The keen-eyed piper was enlivening company, and she was in need of cheering up.

They walked in comfortable silence down the path that skirted the lake. A refreshing breeze blew, causing the water's surface to shimmer in the morning sun, and the harebells to ring delicately, but Phoebe saw or heard none of this. Her thoughts were still on Celeste and Lord Murray.

"You seem troubled by something this morning, Miss Hartwell," the piper commented presently.

"Is it that evident, Mr. Dinsmore? I do apologize," Phoebe said ruefully.

"You're thinking of Miss Laurence and Lord Murray, aren't you?"

"Yes," Phoebe admitted.

"You're not alone in your worries," Dinsmore said forthrightly. "There's no denying Miss Laurence is as beautiful as the wild rowan, but she is not for the Murray."

Phoebe was rather disconcerted by his frankness, and was once again struck by the boldness with which all the members of Lord Murray's household offered their opinions.

They had come to a grassy knoll at the edge of the lake, and Dinsmore spread his plaid over a hummock for Phoebe to sit on. He took a stand behind her and they gazed solemnly over the loch.

"It does seem to me at times that Miss Laurence and Lord Murray are not suited," Phoebe commented at length, "but they are betrothed. There is nothing we can do."

"It is plain to me the Daoine Shi' sent Miss Laurence," Dinsmore muttered.

"The Daoine Shi'?" Phoebe enquired, turning to look at Dinsmore questioningly.

"The Men of Peace," Dinsmore translated. "They are faery folk who live underground and are well-known for their mischief. They are happy enough little folk until the time comes when they decide someone is happier. Then there's the devil to pay though they mean no real harm and fancy a bit of fun. I ken they decided we were too happy at Abermaise, and they hae sent Miss Laurence tae make their mischief. I kenned it frae the moment I saw her een, for green is the colour o' the faery folk," he finished, his brogue, which he could lay aside at will, creeping back into his speech as he became more emotional.

"Men of Peace is a strange name for them," Phoebe commented, but she did not challenge his belief. She thought of Celeste's changeable green eyes and how often she herself had thought there was something of the sprite about her friend. Yet surely no real harm would come to Castle Abermaise even if the Daoine Shi' had sent Celeste to cut up their peace.

"Miss Laurence is young and unused to your ways, but she will learn," Phoebe ventured to say, although she was not fully convinced of her own words. "In time you will become comfortable with each other."

"There's those wha belong and those wha dinna," Dinsmore said with finality. "Miss Laurence doesna. The Murray wad hae done better to choose you."

Phoebe looked at Dinsmore in some alarm, wondering if the sharp-eyed piper had divined her secret, but his face revealed nothing.

"I am not Scottish either."

"You maun hae *some* Scots bluid in you," Dinsmore argued. "You hae red hair and you like the pipes. Nor do you scorn the Daoine Shi'."

"My grandmother was Scottish," Phoebe admitted, "but," she added mischievously, "she might have been a Lowlander."

"Ah, weel," Dinsmore sighed. "One canna hae everything."

They remained a few minutes longer, lost in their separate reflections. Phoebe had thought that perhaps her own feelings for Lord Murray had made her perceive a problem between Celeste and Lord Murray where none had existed, but if Dinsmore had sensed it as well, truly something was amiss. Perhaps she should speak to Celeste about her engagement. Although they normally shared everything, Phoebe had avoided the subject for as long as she could, her own feelings for Lord Murray making the topic a painful one.

UPON HER RETURN to the castle, Phoebe searched for Celeste, planning to speak to her before she lost her courage, but her friend was still closeted with Lady Melville. She decided to wait in the garden, and went back downstairs, where she found yet another argument in process between Mrs. Baird and Balneaves.

Phoebe wondered sometimes how the castle ran as smoothly as it did with the constant friction between the two.

"I'll nae gie the kelpies reason tae dae me onie skaith," the housekeeper was saying, "'an they will an we tak their food."

"It is Miss Laurence's wish to have fish from the lake included on the menu," Balneaves proclaimed. "It is an order."

"Wha richt hae you tae gie me orders," Mrs. Baird retorted, "you Hieland ferlie."

Balneaves looked down his long nose at the indignant housekeeper. "I must if you cannot understand English sufficiently to converse with Miss Laurence."

"I ken Inglish weel. It's nae my faut Miss Laurence dinnae ken Scots."

"When Miss Laurence becomes Lady Murray where will you be?" the butler asked maliciously.

Mrs. Baird spied Phoebe as she hesitated at the bottom of the stairs. "I canna offend the keplies, can I, Miss Hartweel?"

Thanks to her discussion with Dinsmore, Phoebe guessed that the kelpies must be some sort of water spirit to whom the lake fish belonged. What Dinsmore had said about Celeste gave her an idea.

"Mr. Dinsmore tells me Miss Laurence was sent by the faeries. If it is true they sent her, the kelpies would surely accept her as one of their own and would not mind if she were to eat their fish," Phoebe suggested logically.

Mrs. Baird and Balneaves both looked much struck by this argument.

"I hadna thocht 'o that," Mrs. Baird admitted.

Balneaves gave Phoebe a look of respect before he withdrew. Phoebe remained to speak to Mrs. Baird, hoping to dissipate any feelings of resentment she might still be harbouring towards Celeste.

"I am sure Miss Laurence did not mean to trespass upon your sensibilities by giving orders through Balneaves," Phoebe said in a conciliatory voice. "She is very young and does not understand." Phoebe vaguely registered that she seemed to be making many excuses of late for her friend.

Mrs. Baird allowed herself to be somewhat placated. "It's true shes na mair than a bit lassie. But," she added, "you ken me fine."

"I am older," Phoebe said, admitting to herself that the real reason was that she made the effort to understand Mrs. Baird and Celeste did not.

The housekeeper left to give orders regarding the fish, and Phoebe went back upstairs to see if Celeste had finished with Lady Melville. She would have to explain the proper procedures to follow before Celeste made things more strained between Mrs. Baird and Balneaves.

She discovered Celeste in her chamber, leafing through *Lady of the Lake*.

"Why cannot Mrs. Baird speak English like the other servants," Celeste complained, when Phoebe informed her of the problem she had caused.

"The others sometimes speak Gaelic, and you do not understand that, either," Phoebe commented, "but that does not upset you."

"Yes, but when they speak to *me* they speak in English," Celeste replied unarguably. She laid her book down and got up, pacing restlessly. "I did not mean to cause problems in Lord Murray's domestic staff," she said penitently. "But it would be so much easier if Mrs. Baird would speak like everyone else."

She went to look through one of the narrow windows, clasping her hands behind her back and staring out pensively.

"Celeste, do you truly think you will be happy here?" Phoebe ventured to ask, sensing that now might be a good chance to broach the subject. "I do not think it is quite what you had expected. Are you positive you wish to spend all your life here in the Highlands? You will if you marry Lord Murray. You *do* realize that?"

Celeste turned from the window and spoke thoughtfully.

"No, it is not quite what I had expected, but once we are actually married I shall tell Lord Murray we must spend at least six months in London each year."

"But Lord Murray has many duties here," Phoebe objected. "His kinsmen demand much of his time. I doubt he would be willing to be absent so much of the year.''

''Pooh. He can leave the running of his lands to his bailiff, and surely his kinsmen can get along without him for a few months.''

''But if you should change your mind and not marry Lord Murray you could return to London for another Season. You could undoubtedly meet a gentleman who lives in London all year, or who has estates nearer Town. Would you not like that better?''

Celeste looked at Phoebe in surprise. ''Then he would not be a Highlander. And Lord Murray would probably return to England and offer for Olivia. After all we did to win his attention I could not bear to have that happen.''

Phoebe did not attempt to remonstrate further with Celeste, realizing the younger girl simply did not understand Lord Murray's strong feeling of duty and devotion to his lands and people. But persuasive as Phoebe knew Celeste could be, she doubted Celeste could ever cause Lord Murray to fail in what he perceived to be his duty. Such a fundamental difference in outlook was bound to lead to unhappiness for both.

LORD MURRAY CONSIDERED his fiancée thoughtfully as he sipped his wine at supper. She looked quite charming in her simple primrose gown, a wreath of flowers in her hair, but her beauty was marred by the bored expression on her face. He feared she was not finding the Highlands to be what she had imagined from reading *Lady of the Lake,* and it was apparent she missed Town entertainments. She had little interest in the simple occupations they had to offer at Castle Abermaise. It worried him too that his servants and kinsmen seemed to avoid her. They were not taking to her, nor she to them, he added fairly. He sighed, hoping it would not be long before she informed him they would not suit.

Miss Hartwell looked up at the sound of his sigh and he smiled, feeling a warmth spread through him at her answering one. He had recently had to question his original motives in choosing to offer for Miss Laurence. Had he not known from the beginning he and Miss Laurence would never suit, at heart? He could have offered for Lady Sheridan, or any one of several other eligible ladies. Had he, in his unconscious mind, always intended to suggest Miss Hartwell accompany his betrothed to Perthshire? And if so, what did that say about his character—that he would be willing to risk both Miss Laurence's and Miss Hartwell's happiness, not to mention young Atwood's, just to have Phoebe near him?

"What are you thinking of so seriously?" his aunt enquired. "You are neglecting our guests."

"I am sorry," he apologized, casting about in his mind for an excuse and remembering a letter he had received that morning.

"I was thinking of Miles. He is to join us here to-morrow. Miles Huntsford is my cousin," he explained to Miss Laurence and Miss Hartwell.

"Another cousin?" Celeste asked, a marked lack of interest in her voice.

Lord Murray grinned, realizing she was referring to his more distant "cousins" below stairs.

"This cousin is my uncle Malcolm's son," he explained. "He has been travelling on the Continent and is but recently come home to Scotland. He lives with my aunt and uncle in Edinburgh, but is accustomed to spending his summers here. I think you will find his company enjoyable."

He watched his fiancée's eyes brighten with interest at the prospect of a visit from this "real" cousin.

"It will be a pleasure to see Miles again," Lady Melville commented. "He always knows the latest fashions and news."

Lord Murray opened his mouth to tell his guests more about Miles when the sound of bagpipes invaded the room.

"Do not tell me Dinsmore has the right to play in the evening, too," Miss Laurence said exasperatedly.

Lord Murray laughed aloud at the expression on Miss Laurence's face. There was no love lost between his piper and fiancée.

"No. This will not be a usual occurrence, I promise, Miss Laurence," he said aloud. "My kinsmen are having a dance in the Great Hall this evening. Would you care to join them?''

"Oh, yes, do let us," Miss Hartwell answered quickly before Miss Laurence could speak.

Lord Murray saw Miss Laurence frown at Miss Hartwell and give a slight shake of her head, but Miss Hartwell pretended not to see, and the matter was settled.

PHOEBE AND CELESTE met Lord Murray in the drawing room after supper when they had dressed for the dance. They were not sure what the occasion was, so they had chosen to wear pretty but simple gowns of yellow striped silk. Lord Murray was resplendent in a claret-coloured coat, dark brown kerseymere breeches and elegant clocked stockings. Celeste hardly glanced at Lord Murray, and Phoebe wondered how she could be so impervious to his dark good looks.

On their way down the stairs Phoebe felt an excitement rise in her breast as the pipe music became louder. There were two other pipers besides Dinsmore this evening, and the wild seductive music made Phoebe long to join the dancers. As the three were ushered to chairs, Phoebe watched the couples enviously, amazed when the men swung their partners clear off the floor so the women extended horizontally with the stone floor.

"What kind of a dance is that?" Celeste asked her. "I should be afraid to be dropped."

"I do not know," Phoebe responded, "but I think it looks like fun."

"It is a reel," Lord Murray answered, overhearing Celeste's question. "Would you care to try it, Miss Laurence?"

"No, thank you," Celeste responded, looking horrified at the idea.

Phoebe hoped that Lord Murray would ask her, but he evidently felt he must remain at the side of his betrothed, for he did not ask. She was watching the dancers wistfully when one of Lord Murray's kinsmen came up to her, and with a twinkle in his eye, asked her if she would care to stand up with him.

"Thank you, Mr. Spalding, but I am not familiar with the steps," she protested halfheartedly.

"I am sure Spalding will be willing to teach you, so don't hesitate on that account," Lord Murray responded, his eyes daring her to accept.

Phoebe could not resist the challenge and rose, putting her small hand into the Scotsman's large one. He led her to the edge of the floor where he explained the steps to her and took her slowly through them. Phoebe caught on quickly and they joined the others on the floor. As Lord Murray's guest, Phoebe expected to be treated with more caution, at least, and was surprised when her partner began to swing her about as though her weight was no more than a feather. When she first felt her feet leaving the ground, she had a moment of fright in case she should fall on the stones, but her fears quickly vanished in the exhilaration of the wild dance and she entered wholeheartedly into the spirit of the reel. She was sorry when it ended and Mr. Spalding returned her, flushed and disarrayed, to Lord Murray and Celeste.

"How could you," whispered Celeste. "Were you not frightened?"

"At first, but you cannot imagine the feeling. You should try it."

"No, thank you," Celeste replied. "I prefer a nice English cotillion."

Now the women left the floor and swords were placed crossways on the stones. Three kilted Scotsmen performed the sword dance while the others watched. Phoebe was fascinated, but Celeste whispered that the bagpipes were giving her a headache and that she wished to leave. She repeated her wish to Lord Murray, who nodded his agreement. Phoebe, disappointed, stood up to leave as well, but Lord Murray told her that if she wished to remain, he would entrust her to the care of Dinsmore.

Although part of her enjoyment of the evening left with Lord Murray, Phoebe had a wonderful time, and it was not until the wee hours of the morning that Dinsmore escorted her upstairs.

Upon entering her bedchamber, she discovered Celeste asleep on top of her bedcovers. Evidently she had wished to talk to her, had dismissed Sara and then fallen asleep waiting. Phoebe stood looking at her friend, shading her candle so that the light would not fall on Celeste's face and waken her. How exquisite her face was in repose, so young and innocent. At this moment she looked more like an angel than the mischievous sprite she sometimes appeared in the daytime.

Suddenly, Phoebe had a vision of how Celeste's face would appear in repose ten years from now if she married Lord Murray. It would no longer be smooth and beautiful, but lined with the marks of discontent and boredom.

Phoebe blew out her candle and began to undress herself in the dark, thinking. The betrothal could not be allowed to continue. She saw only too clearly that if it did, two people she cared for very deeply would become excessively unhappy.

Yet how could she stop it? Her attempts to talk to Celeste seriously about her engagement to Lord Murray had failed. Celeste was determined to see herself as the heroine of a Scottish epic, and also to make a match that would be the envy of Olivia and the rest of Society. The only way to end the matter would be through Lord Murray. Would that serve? Could she win his affections from Celeste? She felt she could, for she had sensed his admiration of her. She could at least try.

As Phoebe slipped into the bed next to her friend, she felt some qualms about her plan. Would it not be a betrayal of Celeste in one sense? Yet surely to allow the betrothal to continue and end in marriage would be a worse betrayal, would it not?

CHAPTER EIGHT

IN HER DILEMMA over whether to try to win Lord Murray's affections from Celeste or not, Phoebe had forgotten that Lord Murray's cousin, Miles Huntsford, was to arrive the following day. Celeste, however, had not.

"Lord Murray failed to mention how old his cousin is. I wonder what he looks like. Do you suppose he is dark like Lord Murray?" Celeste eagerly speculated.

"I could not hazard a guess," Phoebe responded, her conscience feeling partially relieved by Celeste's interest in the visitor. Surely if Celeste cared deeply for Lord Murray she would not be so curious about another gentleman.

However, Celeste's excitement was infectious, and when Miles Huntsford arrived early that afternoon, Phoebe was almost as eager to meet him as was Celeste. Her first thought upon seeing him was that here was Mr. Scott's Malcolm Graeme come to life. He was tall and slender, with a muscular frame and wavy fair hair, and Phoebe felt all he needed to complete the picture was a belted plaid.

Miles Huntsford first greeted Lady Melville, and then Lord Murray presented Celeste to him.

"So this is your choice for your lady, Robert?" he asked. He took Celeste's hands and looked at her with open admiration. "But she is much too beautiful to be immured in a lonely Highland castle. Indeed, Robert, the thought is positively Gothic."

Celeste smiled and returned his greeting warmly. Mr. Huntsford's light banter was very much to her taste.

Nor did Mr. Huntsford ignore Phoebe. "Miss Hartwell, I am indeed charmed to make your acquaintance," he said when she was presented to him. "Your presence adds a glow to Castle Abermaise that was heretofore lacking."

"Are you referring to the colour of my hair or my presence?" Phoebe asked mischievously.

"Your beauty and your presence both, of course," he replied with a twinkle. "But your hair is not the least of your beauty."

During supper Miles Huntsford kept them all entertained with stories of his adventures on the Continent, not forgetting to include details of the latest fashions and dances. They were particularly interested in his descriptions of the new German dance called the waltz.

After the meal the men did not remain long talking over their port, but joined the three women within the half-hour. Lady Melville dozed by the fire she always had lit, contriving to look dignified even while asleep. Miles Huntsford promptly attached himself to Celeste, and Lord Murray was left to converse with Phoebe, to her great pleasure.

Phoebe and Lord Murray were talking companionably when a peal of laughter from Celeste caused them to turn and look at her. Celeste's whole attention was on Mr. Huntsford, and her very being seemed to sparkle. It was clear she was in a happier mood than she had been in for a long time. Phoebe involuntarily shook her head at Celeste's behaviour. Should Celeste conceive a liking for Miles Huntsford, Phoebe would be the first one to promote it, but for Celeste to show her preference for another's company when her betrothed was in the same room was not at all the thing.

"I hope it is not my fiancée who causes you to shake your head so reprovingly," Lord Murray said, reclaiming Phoebe's attention. "I imagine Miss Laurence is starved for Town gossip. I am sure she means no harm."

Phoebe turned back to Lord Murray, unsure how to respond. Now was her chance to indicate how unfitted for Highland life Celeste was, but Phoebe could not bring herself to say anything disparaging about her friend.

"Celeste does miss London," she said carefully. "It will be quite an adjustment for her to live so far away year-round."

She thought of Dinsmore's words and gave a little laugh. "Dinsmore is convinced Celeste was sent by the Men of Peace to make mischief and disturb the happiness of your Castle."

Lord Murray glanced at Celeste again and joined Phoebe in her laughter. "Miss Laurence *has* always put me in mind of a sea nymph," he confessed, "but what makes Dinsmore think she was sent by the Daoine Shi'?"

"Well," Phoebe explained, "at first it was her green eyes that gave him the idea, but then when he heard that she had ordered fish to be included on the menu, he became convinced that only someone sent by faeries would request such a thing."

"I can well imagine the scene that must have transpired below stairs," Lord Murray said with a chuckle.

Phoebe laughed again and recounted the episode including the happy ending.

Lord Murray joined in her laughter at the completion of the tale, and then his face sobered.

"I think Miss Laurence is not completely comfortable with our way of life here. I fear she has not found Mr. Scott's brave Highlands, but what must seem to her a parody. I hope she will not hesitate to call off the betrothal if she comes to believe we should not suit," he dared to say, hoping Miss Hartwell would repeat his remarks to her friend.

"I think Celeste is not sure what she desires at the moment," Phoebe replied. "It is true her interest in the Highlands stemmed from reading the poem. I only hope," she said, trying to give Lord Murray a hint that he might have to be the one to take the initiative, "that she can come to distinguish between her dreams and reality before it is too late."

For a moment they sat in silence. As Phoebe covertly watched Lord Murray she felt an almost tangible pull between them. She realized she was being provided with the opportunity to activate her plan of winning Lord Murray's affections away from Celeste and turning them to herself. But now that she had the chance to flirt with Lord Murray she was not precisely sure how to go about it. She thought of Olivia's tactics when dealing with her admirers and gave Lord Murray what she felt was a bold smile.

Lord Murray smiled warmly at her in return, and looked at her intently, so softly beautiful in the candlelight she was. He had a sudden urge to reach out and run his hands through her fiery hair. He wondered what her response would be if he did—did she have a passionate nature under the calm front she presented to the world?

Abruptly Lord Murray recalled Wilfred Atwood and he became puzzled by Miss Hartwell's behaviour. If it were not for Atwood, he would think she was trying to set up a flirtation with him. But while he felt no surprise to see Miss Laurence flirt with his cousin while technically engaged to him, he could not credit such discourteous conduct to Miss Hartwell. To flout convention was not in her nature. Perhaps his popularity in London had given him an exaggerated opinion of himself. He must be imagining things. Whichever was the case, to pursue her would be madness. Both he and she were engaged to others. Until that ceased to be, he must not allow himself to think of Miss Hartwell.

As a diversion, Lord Murray rang for one of his kinsmen who played the harp. For all parties concerned it would be much safer to end the tête-à-têtes and share in a common entertainment.

WHEN PHOEBE AND CELESTE walked to their chambers at the end of the evening, Phoebe felt that her plan was off to a good beginning although it had not progressed as quickly as she had for a moment thought it might. She knew Lord Murray was attracted to her, yet he had drawn away. Had she been too bold? Not bold enough? Was it Celeste? He had not seemed unduly upset by her coquettish behaviour towards his cousin.

"I asked you what you thought of Miles Huntsford," Celeste repeated for the second time. "You are wool-gathering."

They had come to the door of Phoebe's room and entered together.

"I am sorry," Phoebe said, wrenching her thoughts away from Lord Murray. "I like Mr. Huntsford very much. I think he looks like Malcolm Graeme."

"You noticed that, too?" Celeste asked, sitting gracefully on a chair by the fire. "And he has such address. Much more than Lord Murray. Lord Murray is too serious.

"Do you know, Phoebe," Celeste added thoughtfully, "perhaps I made a mistake to accept Lord Murray."

"Not a mistake," Phoebe said as her maid helped her out of her gown, Celeste's words causing her heart to leap with hope. "You merely agreed to visit Castle Abermaise in order to determine whether you could like living here. If you find you cannot, you can break it off, with no one outside the castle and our families any the wiser."

"That is true," Celeste said. She watched idly as Phoebe prepared for bed, a dreamy look on her face. "I wonder if Mr. Huntsford ever travels to London," she said.

"You should not be thinking so much of another gentleman when you are still betrothed to Lord Murray," Phoebe felt obliged to say.

Celeste smiled, her beautiful eyes unreadable in the firelight. "Don't be so stuffy," she said lightly, after which she rose and went to her own chamber, singing softly to herself.

Phoebe went to bed happier than she had been since she had arrived at the castle. How much more simple it would all be should Celeste fall in love with Miles Huntsford and break off the engagement herself.

LORD MURRAY and Miles Huntsford remained together in the drawing room after Lady Melville,
Phoebe and Celeste retired, sharing a bottle of excellent French brandy Miles had brought from the
Continent.

"I notice you fully approve of my intended bride,"
Lord Murray commented rather dryly to his cousin.
It had not escaped him that Miles was as guilty as
Miss Laurence in trying to set up a flirtation.

Miles grinned unrepentantly.

"I approve of Miss Laurence, but not of your betrothal."

"That is plain speaking."

Lord Murray rose from his chair and went to stand
before the fireplace. He thoughtfully regarded his
cousin, who relaxed lazily in an armchair, his legs
stretched out before him. Lord Murray supposed he
should be angry with Miles for so blatantly trying to
steal his fiancée, but he could not be. Nor did he feel
piqued that Miss Laurence so obviously preferred his
cousin to himself. If he felt anything, he decided, it
was relief.

Suddenly he threw his head back and laughed.
Miles looked at him quizzically, and he picked up the
decanter, pouring them both another drink.

"To Miss Laurence," he said. That was as close as
he would come to saying Miles might steal his betrothed with his blessing. To say it more clearly
would be to insult Miss Laurence.

Miles drank and then proposed a toast of his own.

"To Miss Hartwell," he said, his eyes twinkling knowingly.

OVER THE NEXT FEW DAYS Phoebe was amazed at how easily her hopes were being realized. Miles Huntsford was apparently as drawn to Celeste as she was to him. They spent most of their time together, riding, walking and talking of his travels abroad. Lord Murray was busy with estate business, and Phoebe occupied herself by assisting Lady Melville with her duties and occasionally accompanying Celeste and Lord Huntsford on their rides and walks.

She wondered a little at Miles Huntsford so openly showing his interest in Celeste when she was technically betrothed to his cousin and then realized shamefully that she had no right to criticize. What was she trying to do but win Lord Murray from her best friend? Could it be that Mr. Huntsford had already ascertained how unsuited Celeste and Lord Murray were for each other?

Phoebe was quite amused to see how well Miles Huntsford understood Celeste and used his knowledge to win her attention. One night soon after his arrival he appeared at supper in full Highland dress. Although he was not a large man, like Lord Murray, the kilt and hose suited his muscular frame, and even Phoebe looked at him admiringly.

"I can see I have made an error never to wear the traditional attire of my countrymen," Lord Murray said to Phoebe as he took a seat next to her in the drawing room after supper. "Is it the philabeg or the man?" he asked, noting Celeste's almost awed expression as she looked at his cousin.

"I must confess Scottish dress is very impressive," Phoebe replied. "Something about it makes a gentleman look, well, different," she finished lamely, unable to put into acceptable words that the costume seemed to make a gentleman appear more strong and masculine. "I have often admired Dinsmore's dress, too," she added, lest Lord Murray think she also was captivated by Mr. Huntsford.

"If I wore a belted plaid would you look at me as Miss Laurence looks at Miles?" Lord Murray asked so softly that Phoebe was not sure she had heard him aright, but the expression on his face told her she had.

Phoebe made no immediate reply, her mind conjuring up an image of Lord Murray in bonnet, plaid, kilt, sporran and hose. The picture was so vivid that she felt her cheeks grow warm.

"You are sitting too near the fire," Lady Melville said, noticing the colour even from her chair halfway across the room. "Come and sit next to me," she invited, and Phoebe was mercifully able to escape without having to give Lord Murray a reply.

Lord Murray watched as the rosy hue in Phoebe's cheeks gradually subsided. He was not wrong. Miss Hartwell was attracted to him. Had she, like him, realized that she had made a mistake in her betrothal? Had she come to care for him in a way she did not care for Atwood? He felt instinctively that she had. Soon Miss Laurence would ask to be freed and he could speak to Miss Hartwell.

WHEN CELESTE HEARD Lady Melville invite Phoebe to sit by her, she wondered guiltily if she had been failing in common civility towards the older woman these past few days. Certainly she had allowed little time for her, spending every moment she could with Mr. Huntsford.

"Remembering your social duties, Miss Laurence?" Miles Huntsford asked.

Celeste turned to face him, once again disconcerted by the ease with which he read her thoughts.

"Yes, I am afraid I have not been as attentive as I might," she admitted.

Miles smiled at her, and Celeste felt another thrill go down her spine. All thoughts of neglect vanished. How handsome Mr. Huntsford was in his kilt and all! That was how a Highland lord should look, not all plain and ordinary like Lord Murray in his stuffy evening clothes. As she absorbed Mr. Huntsford's romantic appearance like a rare perfume, she knew for certain that she would be ending her betrothal with Lord Murray very soon.

Miles Huntsford was aware of Celeste's almost reverent admiration, and was at once amused and touched. One of the things that most appealed to him about Miss Laurence was her youthful romanticism. He played his part to the hilt for her benefit, but he could not say that he did not understand her need to follow her heart. The same longing for romance and adventure was what had driven him to travel. He would never be a settled landowner like his cousin. Robert was a fine fellow, but rather dull. The quicksilver child he had chosen was not for him. The time had arrived for Celeste to be awakened from childhood, but Robert was not the man to do the job. Not that he had to worry about his cousin, Miles thought. Clearly *his* affections lay elsewhere. He glanced briefly at Lord Murray and back to Celeste. He sensed he had not much longer to wait before she would end the betrothal.

THE FOLLOWING MORNING while on his way to his bailiff, Lord Murray encountered Phoebe clad in her walking dress.

"Are you setting out for a walk, Miss Hartwell? May I accompany you?" he asked impulsively, thinking how pleasant it would be to share some quiet time out-of-doors in her company.

Phoebe agreed, also happy at the prospect of some moments alone with Lord Murray. Or almost alone, she amended, as they left the castle, the ever-present gillie following at a distance. Phoebe started down her usual path, but Lord Murray stopped her and led her to one she had not seen before.

"I would like to show you my favourite spot," he said. "The view of the loch is incomparable."

They made fairly slow progress over the less-travelled path, and Lord Murray had to assist her over some rough places, but they finally reached their destination. He led her to some rocks poised precipitously over the lake, and Phoebe sank down gratefully.

However, when she surveyed the spectacular view, she knew Lord Murray had found a beautiful spot and that the difficult walk had been well worth it. Directly beneath them the lake lapped greedily at the shore showering them lightly with its spray. Thick forests loomed darkly to their left, and to their right fields dotted with white sheep spread beyond the far shore.

They sat silently for a long while and Phoebe was startled when she heard Lord Murray's voice.

"Hold still a moment, there is a spider on your shoulder."

Phoebe obediently froze, having a strong dislike of spiders. She felt Lord Murray's hand brush her skin through her light pelisse.

"It is gone," he said reassuringly, but he did not remove his hand. Instead, he caressed her shoulder lightly, and then gently turned her so that she was facing him.

Time seemed suspended for a long moment as they looked into each other's eyes, seeing there what neither of them had yet dared to confess.

"Phoebe," Lord Murray said softly, speaking her given name.

Phoebe's lips parted in unconscious invitation. She heard Lord Murray draw a sharp breath, and then he leaned forward, covering her lips with his. His kiss was soft and slow, and she returned it, tentatively at first, and then with awakening passion. As she began to feel that she was melting into his very being the memory of certain facts intruded and she pulled abruptly away.

"Please Lord Murray, this will not serve while you are betrothed to Celeste," she protested.

Lord Murray did not attempt to retain his hold on her.

"No, it will not," he agreed, his eyes still dark with passion. "Not while neither of us are free to follow our hearts. We shall wait until circumstances are such that we may embrace with no shame or guilt."

That was as close to a declaration of his feelings as Lord Murray felt it was proper for him to make now, but he wanted Phoebe to understand his intentions were serious. He took her hand in his, pressing it affectionately, and pulled her up. They had best return to the castle before his feelings overcame propriety and he kissed her again. For the first time since he had set out on his search for a bride he felt he would win the lady he had wanted most. He was sure Phoebe had understood that he had been referring to her engagement to Atwood as well as his own to Miss Laurence, and that she would break hers off when she returned to London. He only wished she did not have to wait so long to do so.

Feeling that they were in perfect agreement and that each one understood what could not yet be said, they began the walk back. Phoebe was a little abashed when she saw the gillie was still following them and realized he must have observed their kiss, although he gave no sign he had seen anything. Lord Murray noticed her apprehension and smiled at her reassuringly.

As they neared the castle, Phoebe was surprised to spot a carriage being unloaded before the entrance.

"Did you invite more guests?" she asked Lord Murray.

"No, I am not expecting anyone. I wonder who it can be?" he replied, as they quickened their steps.

The carriage itself gave them no hint as to the identity of the visitors, for it was a hired one. Filled with curiosity they went up the steps to the castle. The great door swung open as they approached, revealing three people standing just inside the huge stone-paved Hall. One of them came forward, smiling broadly, to greet them.

"Lord Murray. We have been on our excursion to Loch Katrine and were so near your castle that we knew you would never forgive us if we did not stop and make a visit."

CHAPTER NINE

OLIVIA'S SMILE BECAME BROADER as she saw the look of surprise and shock that flashed across Phoebe's face. Lord Murray, however, evinced no surprise, but strode forward to welcome Olivia, her mother and brother with apparent sincerity.

Olivia had been furious and mortified when Lord Murray had left London without offering for her. When she had heard from her father that Phoebe and Celeste were going to stay at Castle Abermaise that summer, she had come to the unpalatable conclusion that for reasons she could not fathom, Lord Murray planned to marry one of them.

After Olivia's boasts of Lord Murray's interest in her, the comments of Society when no announcement had appeared in the *Gazette* had not been kind. To end the gossip, Olivia had put it about that she had been invited to stay at Castle Abermaise after her excursion to Lake Katrine. She gambled that Lord Murray would have no choice but to welcome them, particularly since he had stayed at her father's home just the month before. Her mother had not discouraged her plans, and Wilfred's objections had easily been overridden.

Olivia noted that Lord Murray was busy talking to her mother and took the opportunity to approach Phoebe.

"I knew you and Miss Laurence would be pleased to see me," she said sweetly, kissing her with apparent affection. "How delightful it will be for the three of us to enjoy a visit here together.

"Where is Miss Laurence?" she finished, wondering where the younger girl could be since the two friends were almost always together.

As if in answer to her question, Celeste and Miles Huntsford entered the castle. Lord Murray presented Olivia and her family to his cousin, and Olivia looked at Miles Huntsford speculatively. Should she consider him a candidate for marriage as well as Lord Murray? He was not of as high a rank, for Lord Murray had introduced him as the Honourable Miles Huntsford, but he might have estates and wealth that would help her overlook that flaw. He was well enough looking, although she personally preferred Lord Murray's dark rugged visage to Mr. Huntsford's more polished appearance. She would have her maid make enquiries about Mr. Huntsford among the other servants and see what she could discover about his circumstances.

Olivia kissed Celeste's cheek and was pleased to see a sulky look enter that young lady's eyes. She wondered which of the two friends Lord Murray had either offered for or was thinking of offering for. Well, there was time enough to find out. She planned to stay as long as Phoebe and Celeste did, or until Lord Murray offered for *her* hand.

Olivia turned back to the others. She was now ready to remove the stains of travel and put on a more becoming gown. Noticing the red-haired man in Highland dress Lord Murray had presented as his piper standing nearby, she addressed him with authority.

"You shall show me to my rooms," she ordered, ignoring the anger that flared in his eyes.

"This way, please," Dinsmore said, the necessity to be polite to guests restraining his natural indignation at being spoken to as though he were a footman.

Olivia followed Dinsmore cheerfully, quite satisfied with herself.

THE ATWOODS did not take dinner at noon, for they were resting from their journey, but all the guests appeared at supper. Olivia looked extremely beautiful in a yellow silk evening gown with a very low décolletage that displayed her generous curves.

Phoebe smiled at her "friend" and politely enquired after her health, thinking that the Atwoods' arrival boded no good. Things were never pleasant around Olivia. She wondered how the others felt about the addition to their company, and glanced about the table, trying to read their expressions. She had no success with Lord Murray as he was carefully concealing any adverse reaction he may have had. Lady Melville wore a mask of perfect politeness. Celeste was not bothering to hide the evidence that she was downright sullen, and Mr. Huntsford appeared amused, as usual.

"Lady Atwood, how do you find Scotland in your travels so far?" Miles enquired politely of Olivia's mother just as Phoebe's glance rested upon him.

"Oh, it is wonderful," Olivia declared before her mother could reply. "The countryside is so beautiful. Just as Mr. Scott described in his poem. I simply adore everything Scottish."

"Indeed," Miles commented, adding mischievously, "Miss Laurence would not agree."

Olivia looked at Celeste as though astounded. "Oh, how could you not? Scotland is a fascinating country."

Celeste looked daggers at Miles Huntsford and attempted to defend herself.

"I agree that Scotland is a beautiful country, but the customs here are very different and it takes time to become accustomed to them."

Phoebe could almost see Olivia mentally calculating how much to her advantage it would be to defend everything Scottish since Celeste had admitted she was not as enchanted as she should be. Olivia's next words confirmed Phoebe's suspicion.

"I am persuaded you at least must agree with me, Miss Hartwell. I can see Scotland has done you both wonders. You look to be in robust health, and Miss

Laurence's complexion is quite blooming, without a sign of spots.''

Celeste, who had never been plagued with spots and was angry at the implication she had been, particularly in front of Mr. Huntsford, looked stormy. Phoebe hastily intervened telling Olivia she was "too kind," and adroitly drew Lady Atwood into the conversation, forcing Celeste to keep her counsel.

The rest of the supper passed uneventfully but uncomfortably. It was not at all like the meals they had shared in the past. Phoebe was glad when the evening was finally over and they could escape to their bedchambers.

"Why did Olivia have to come and spoil everything?" Celeste complained when they got together for their customary evening visit in Phoebe's room.

"I suppose we should have expected their arrival," Phoebe answered. "We knew she was to travel to Lake Katrine this summer."

"We must think of a way to get rid of her," Celeste proclaimed, throwing herself across Phoebe's bed and staring at the ceiling, frowning in concentration.

Phoebe, knowing Celeste's temper, was made uneasy by her words. "We cannot get rid of Olivia," she said, sitting on the edge of the bed and looking at Celeste seriously. "This is not even our home. The Highlanders have very strict ideas of hospitality and the proper treatment of guests. Did you notice how Dinsmore said nothing when Olivia ordered him to show her her rooms, despite the fact he must have been terribly insulted to be addressed like a servant?"

"Oh, I did not mean to order her out of the house or anything of that sort. But there must be a way to make her *want* to leave."

"I cannot think of any, short of your actual marriage to Lord Murray, and even if there were some way to encourage her to leave, good manners forbid it," Phoebe replied. "Promise me that you will abandon your notion, Celeste."

Celeste remained obstinately silent.

"Promise," Phoebe commanded.

"Oh, very well," Celeste agreed grumpily. "But you shall wish to reconsider soon. Did you hear her at supper? 'Oh, Lord Murray, the very air of Scotland improves one's health. Oh, Lord Murray, tartan is so beautiful. Might I have a length of it to have a skirt made? I simply *adore* everything Scottish.' "

"She did rather overplay her hand," Phoebe laughed. "But you encouraged her by confessing there were things about Scotland you did not like."

"That was Mr. Huntsford's fault for bringing up the subject. I believe he did so intentionally," Celeste said, frowning darkly. "At least I was honest, which is more than I can say about her."

Celeste vented her complaints about Olivia a few moments longer and then retired to her own bed-chamber. Although Phoebe had refrained from agreeing out loud, lest she be seeming to endorse

Celeste in her plan, she also felt that if Olivia was to stay on that their sojourn at Castle Abermaise was going to be very different now. The peace was lost, and she doubted it could be restored.

WHEN PHOEBE AND CELESTE went down to breakfast the next morning, they found Olivia already at the table with all the other guests. She gave the friend's toilettes a quick review, and decided hers was the most attractive, smiled and bade them a good-morning. Phoebe and Celeste responded politely and filled their plates at the sideboard.

"It is an interesting custom to have the pipes played in the castle mornings," Lady Atwood commented as Celeste and Phoebe joined the others.

"I do not care for it, myself," Celeste was incautious enough to remark.

"Oh, but I think it an *enchanting* custom!" Olivia exclaimed, glancing at Lord Murray. "I quite adore the sound of bagpipes."

"Don't care overmuch for them m'self," Wilfred said. "Say, what's that you are eating, Miss Hartwell?" he asked, looking curiously at Phoebe's plate of brose.

"A kind of porridge made with oats and barley water and seasoned with salt and butter. We were given some the day we arrived, and I found I quite liked it."

"Oh, is it a traditional Scottish dish?" Olivia enquired. "I must try some."

Lord Murray politely rose and filled her a plate at the sideboard. Olivia thanked him prettily and tasted the mixture.

"But this is quite delicious," she proclaimed. "You say that it is made from oats. Then I should say it is a shame that we eat so few things made from oats in England. They are mostly fed to horses."

"Some say that is why the English have the finest horses and Scotland the finest men," Miles Huntsford interposed, greatly diverted by Olivia's gushings.

Phoebe did not share Lord Huntsford's amusement. Celeste was right, she thought as she watched Olivia eat her brose, praising the divine taste after almost every mouthful. Her determination to extol the virtue of all things Scottish was quite nauseating. And obviously insincere. Phoebe could have sworn she saw a fleeting look of distaste cross Olivia's face when she had first tasted the brose. So Olivia doted on oats, Phoebe thought grimly. She would be sure to mention that to Mrs. Baird. The Highland code of hospitality would demand that Olivia be offered oats at every meal. She would see how she liked that!

Phoebe was suddenly struck by inspiration. Of course! Perhaps there *was* a way to rid themselves of Olivia, as Celeste had suggested, or at least speed her departure. Not only would she inform Mrs. Baird of Olivia's newly acquired devotion to oats, she would also mention to Dinsmore how much Olivia loved the pipes. She might even suggest to the good man that Olivia might like them played outside her chamber door early every morning. Phoebe smiled brilliantly, and Celeste looked at her friend in amazement, wondering what there was about the miserable breakfast to cause her to be so happy.

LORD MURRAY WAS GLAD to escape his new guests after breakfast with the acceptable excuse of pressing estate matters to attend to, although he felt guilty to be so relieved. As a Highlander, he was obliged to welcome his guests and offer them his best hospitality even if they were one of his worst enemies, which of course they were not. The Atwoods had showed him every kindness during his fortnight in London.

Actually, he reflected, he had rather mixed feelings about the Atwoods' arrival. His first thought had been that the visit was a stroke of good fortune, for Phoebe could now break off her engagement to Atwood without having to return to London. But Lady Atwood's and Miss Atwood's company was not congenial, to say the least. He could see, too, that Miss Atwood's presence was upsetting Miss Laurence. His thoughts were interrupted by a tap upon his study door.

"Enter," he called, and Atwood came in. Although it was not yet noon, his attire was already sadly rumpled, and Lord Murray wondered idly how he managed to keep a valet from giving in his notice.

"Like to apologize for Livvy," his visitor said after making his excuses for disturbing his host. "I am sure we have put you out. I tried to tell her it was not the thing to arrive here unannounced, but when m'sister gets the bit between her teeth there's no stopping her," he finished dismally.

"Don't worry about it, you are all more than welcome," Lord Murray assured him politely and sincerely. He quite liked young Atwood, at least.

"Know you're just doing the polite," Wilfred said, looking relieved nonetheless. "I wouldn't want Livvy descending upon me."

"I suppose one might feel that way about one's sister," Lord Murray said understandingly.

"Well, I suppose that could be it. If you're sure we are not putting you out. Must confess it's much more pleasant here than London during the summer, and I am glad to see Miss Hartwell again. Missed her."

Wilfred's confession was a reminder to Lord Murray that his intention was to rob his guest of his beloved betrothed. He was struck once again by Atwood's open countenance and felt the veriest cad. So much for Highland hospitality, he thought wryly. He hoped Miss Hartwell would release Atwood soon as he felt most uncomfortable in his role of the benevolent host.

PHOEBE FOUND the first full day in the company of the Atwoods very different from the ones they had been enjoying. The presence of Lady Atwood and

Olivia prevented them from following their accustomed schedule of activities, since good manners required them to stay with the newer guests. Phoebe would not have minded visiting Wilfred, but he had gone riding with Lord Murray.

Phoebe did have a moment of pleasure at dinner when a servant brought a plate of oatmeal brose and placed it directly before Olivia. At Olivia's look of surprise, Phoebe explained that Mrs. Baird had heard that Miss Atwood had taken a special liking to oatmeal and had ordered the dish prepared specially for her. Olivia made a moue of pleasure and gamely ate the brose while the others helped themselves to the other dishes on the table.

Olivia did not seem to suspect anything, but when the brose reappeared during the first course at supper that evening, Miles Huntsford looked sharply at Phoebe and then slowly broke into a smile. *He knows what I am about,* Phoebe thought, and regarded him with a mixture of defiance and guilt.

Overall, Phoebe found supper trying, for Celeste seemed bent on demonstrating how close she was to the earl. She addressed her every other remark to him, seemed to hang on his every word, and only stopped short of calling him "Robert," which would have proclaimed the existence of their betrothal beyond any question. Phoebe suspected Celeste's sudden interest in Lord Murray was completely motivated by her desire to discompose Olivia, but

Phoebe found her friend's false attentions upsetting nevertheless.

The time spent after supper was even worse, for the men stayed at their port a long time, leaving Phoebe and Celeste to entertain Olivia and Lady Atwood. Celeste had quickly taken the chair next to Lady Melville and Lady Atwood, which left Phoebe to Olivia.

"I am so glad Lord Murray had the kindness to invite you to join us at Castle Abermaise, knowing you could not afford to journey to Lake Katrine with the rest of Society," Olivia said sweetly, for all the world as if it were she who had been first invited.

"Yes, Lord Murray is very kind."

"The Perthshire air must agree with you, for you are looking remarkably well. But I fear you must have been going out without your bonnet and parasol, for I detect several new freckles."

Before Phoebe could reply to this unkind observation, even though Phoebe had to admit it was true, Olivia continued on to a new topic.

"Mr. Huntsford appears to be a most congenial gentleman. Does he also own estates in Perthshire?"

This time Olivia waited for a response, and Phoebe was amused by Olivia's transparent ploy for information regarding Mr. Huntsford's fortune or lack of it.

"I believe Mr. Huntsford resides with his parents in Edinburgh. I am unaware of his owning any estates."

Phoebe was relieved when the gentlemen finally rejoined them and Olivia abandoned her for more exciting company. When Wilfred divined that Phoebe was alone, he came to sit with her and tell her about his latest sporting exploits.

OLIVIA HAD WATCHED Lord Murray carefully that evening both during supper and again when he came into the drawing room. From what her maid had been able to discover so far, Celeste was actually betrothed to Lord Murray, although the engagement had not been officially announced. Olivia had no doubts about her ability to win Lord Murray's affections from Celeste, for Celeste had made her dislike of many Scottish customs plain. Anyone could see nothing was more likely to put Lord Murray off. The Scots were a proud people; she had learned that from reading *Lady of the Lake*. All she had to do was continue to declare her delight in everything Scottish.

Phoebe, however, was another matter. She *did* like Scotland, and Olivia, a sharp observer, had noticed how Phoebe and Lord Murray watched each other when they thought they were unobserved. She had also noted that Lady Melville seemed unusually attached to Phoebe and that Phoebe had somehow managed to gain the authority to actually supervise some of the work in the castle. How she could compete with this unlikely rival she was not sure, since Lord Murray, oddly enough, did not seem overly discouraged by her unenviable looks.

Olivia scanned the occupants of the room again while pretending to go through the sheet music on the pianoforte. Celeste had engaged Lord Murray's ear, Phoebe was listening to Wilfred prose on about something, and her mother was conversing with Mr. Huntsford and Lady Melville. Her roving eye caught Miles Huntsford's attention, and Olivia looked quickly away. She had decided against Miles Huntsford. He was of lower rank than Lord Murray, and, if what Phoebe had said earlier was true, had little wealth. Besides, she felt uncomfortable in his company. She had the distinct impression that he was able to see through her subterfuge and did not care for the feeling it gave her.

Olivia noticed Lord Murray watching Phoebe and Wilfred with keen interest. Could it be that he was jealous of her brother? Slowly, a plan began to form in her mind. If she could persuade Lord Murray that Phoebe and Wilfred had an understanding, she might be able to distract his attention. It would be difficult for anyone to believe a woman could be attached to Wilfred, but Phoebe was not exactly a prize catch and she might be able to point that out, tactfully of course, to Lord Murray.

Olivia decided to act upon her idea immediately. She selected a song from the pile of music and suggested Celeste favour them by performing the piece. Though she knew that Celeste's talent for playing and singing was indifferent, she also knew that Celeste could not refuse. She bade Mr. Huntsford turn the pages for Celeste to forestall Lord Murray's offer, which conveniently left him to herself. She went to sit by the Highland lord.

"Miss Laurence is an excessively lovely and talented young girl, is she not?" Olivia remarked, opening the conversation.

"Yes, indeed she is," Lord Murray agreed.

"Phoebe, now," Olivia continued, "has maturity. I hope I can bring my parents to approve the match between Phoebe and Wilfred. She could be the making of him. He is so awkward and insecure, and Phoebe gives him confidence."

Lord Murray looked a question at Olivia, and she blushed prettily, staring down at her hands folded in her lap.

"Oh, dear, I should not have betrayed them. I hope you will say nothing to Wilfred or Phoebe. It is a sore point with them both, for my parents oppose the match, of course. I must confess," she added, knowing instinctively that her next words would put the seal of authenticity on her words, "that I did not myself at first. But Wilfred was so downcast when Phoebe left London that I was quite concerned that he should make himself ill. But now that we are come to Castle Abermaise, only see how much his spirits have revived with scarce one day in her company. I am convinced it is a love match and I can no longer object.''

Lord Murray's response to Olivia was neutral, but his thoughts were racing. He was no longer blind to Olivia's character and suspected that she had a hidden purpose for revealing the information, but he did not doubt the fundamental truth. Olivia's observations only served to reinforce the conclusion he had had to draw upon observing the couple together. They did indeed appear to be very close. Were Phoebe's feelings for Atwood deeper than he had first thought?

Satisfied that she had succeeded in planting the seeds of doubt, Olivia left Lord Murray's company to take her turn at the pianoforte and display her superior accomplishments. Lord Murray remained where he was, still thinking. Miss Hartwell *must* care for him. He remembered kissing her just two days past, how warmly she had responded, the awakening passion he had felt.

Still, Phoebe had been away from Atwood. Had seeing him again made her change her mind? She did not behave this evening like a person intending to break off a betrothal. It was obvious she was enjoying Atwood's company.

Celeste returned to her place beside Lord Murray, and he was reminded of another complication that had arisen—Celeste's surprisingly possessive attitude towards him. What start had caused her to behave so, particularly given her former apparent preference for his cousin? What a painful muddle the whole affair was. The Daoine Shi' must be very pleased, he reflected.

CHAPTER TEN

PHOEBE FELT A THRILL of guilty pleasure the next morning when the sound of the bagpipes was much louder than usual.

The connecting door to the adjoining chamber was suddenly flung open and Celeste came into Phoebe's room, her hands covering her ears.

"The pipes sound as if they are being played in this very room," she complained.

"I believe Dinsmore heard of Olivia's fondness for pipe music, and like a good hospitable Scotsman, is playing them outside her door for her increased enjoyment."

"Dinsmore never showed such consideration for me when he heard I did *not* care for them," Celeste grumbled.

"I do not think Lord Murray's kinsmen consider you to be a guest, precisely, given your betrothal," Phoebe explained, "but Olivia is a real guest and her preferences must be indulged."

Something in Phoebe's tone of voice made Celeste look closely at her friend. A smile spread slowly over her face as she understood.

"Oh, you are *wicked,* Phoebe," she cried. "I knew you would not fail to think of something."

"I? I did nothing but report a guest's likings," Phoebe said innocently. "Highland courtesy demanded that I do so."

Celeste regarded Phoebe with new admiration. "That explains the oats yesterday, too. I hope your plan works. It is not nearly so pleasant here since Olivia arrived. I cannot believe they have only been here a day and a half. It seems an age."

"At least you cannot say life here is dull."

"Dull?" Celeste repeated. "I never felt it was dull. Everything was perfect until Olivia came."

"I believe your contentment dated from the day Miles Huntsford arrived," Phoebe said rather dryly. "Before that I had the definite impression you were suffering from ennui."

Celeste blushed. "Mr. Huntsford is a very congenial gentleman."

Phoebe gave Celeste a meaningful look but did not tease her further.

"Let us go see how Olivia enjoyed the bagpipes. I daresay everyone should be at breakfast soon. After a few more days of bagpipe music and oatmeal brose perhaps Olivia will set a date for their departure."

BUT AS THE DAYS PASSED Phoebe felt less sanguine about the success of her plan to hasten Olivia's retreat. Olivia was given a plate of oatmeal brose at every meal, and Dinsmore played his pipes directly outside her chamber door every morning, but she was proving difficult to dislodge. Phoebe toyed with the idea of having Olivia's bed removed and replaced with bunches of heather, but decided she did not dare go to quite those lengths.

Olivia's appearance at the castle seemed to have heralded the end of all her hopes and plans, Phoebe thought dismally. And everything had been going so well. She thought of the kiss Lord Murray had given her by the lake barely a sennight past, and found it hard to believe their romantic encounter had ever occurred. Lord Murray had been most remote in his manner towards her since the Atwoods' arrival. The dark eyes that had so often met hers in silent communication were now carefully blank when and if he looked at her, and his voice no longer held that special note of warmth when he spoke to her. The change in his behaviour could simply be attributed to the Atwoods' presence, but then again it might signify a change of heart, and she could not fathom which.

Phoebe sighed deeply and decided to go for a walk. She had been accustomed to walking every morning before the Atwoods had arrived and missed the exercise.

On Phoebe's way downstairs she passed Mrs. Baird and Balneaves in seemingly amicable conversation. The presence of the Atwoods was infecting the whole castle, Phoebe thought. It was not natural for Mrs. Baird and Balneaves to rub along so well.

She noticed the piper sitting in one of the window seats, and impulsively invited him to join her on her walk.

"I hope Miss Atwood is finding the pipe music to her liking?" Dinsmore asked as they strolled along the path.

Something in Dinsmore's voice confirmed Phoebe's suspicion that he, and probably Mrs. Baird as well, knew full well what Phoebe was up to. She was relieved to note there was no censure in his manner. No doubt Dinsmore had not forgiven Olivia for mistaking him for a servant.

"Yes, she has often said how pleased she is," Phoebe answered truthfully. Olivia *was* always careful to say how much she liked them.

"If there is anything else Miss Atwood likes I hope you will so inform Mrs. Baird."

"I shall," Phoebe promised, the rest of what she was going to say dying on her lips as they rounded a curve and came face-to-face with Lord Murray on his way back to the castle. They stopped to exchange greetings, and Dinsmore, with an unreadable expression, said he had forgotten an errand and left the two together.

Lord Murray looked at Phoebe in some consternation. He had been sitting at his favourite spot overlooking the loch this morning trying to puzzle out what to do about her. Phoebe had continued to spend a great deal of time in Atwood's company, and Wilfred's demeanour was certainly not that of a man who had had his troth broken. Moreover, Celeste had continued to behave possessively of him, and should she unaccountably decide to hold him to their engagement, he would have no recourse. He had the most urgent desire to ask Phoebe directly what her feelings were for him, but found he did not dare, fearing what her answer might be.

"Did you wish to walk any farther, Miss Hartwell?" he enquired, his voice sounding flat and cold even to himself.

"No, thank you, Lord Murray. It is time I turned back," Phoebe replied to Lord Murray's commonplace words, her voice equally devoid of emotion. What had happened to change things so, she thought miserably as they walked back in silence.

THAT EVENING Phoebe joined the others at the supper table, wishing she had pleaded the headache and avoided another miserable evening. Celeste was next to Lord Murray, eating some venison with apparent relish. Only Olivia, who was picking at her generous plate of brose, seemed to have as little appetite as Phoebe herself. Celeste, noticing Olivia's halfhearted attempts to eat her brose, turned to her sweetly.

"Is the oatmeal brose not to your liking this evening, Miss Atwood? I am sure Mrs. Baird would instruct the cook to prepare a new mixture if something is amiss."

"Oh, no Miss Laurence, it is quite delicious, as usual," Olivia replied, rallying and taking a more generous spoonful. "You must try some."

"No, thank you. I do not care overmuch for dishes made of oatmeal," Celeste responded, helping herself to some fish.

"It appears there are many things in Scotland you do not care for, Miss Laurence. I wonder that you remain," Olivia said rather tartly.

"Oh, but there are some Scottish things I like very much indeed," Celeste replied, looking significantly at Lord Murray.

Phoebe choked on her bite of partridge. Celeste's implication could not have been more clear. She might as well have openly announced her betrothal to Lord Murray. Phoebe tried to catch Celeste's eye, but her friend carefully avoided looking her way.

"I say, am I to wish you happy?" Wilfred enquired of Lord Murray, thinking perhaps he had been remiss in his manners.

Lord Murray, looking as stunned as Phoebe, said nothing, but Celeste quickly answered for him.

"Thank you, Mr. Atwood. It is unofficial as yet, but I know you will keep my news in confidence. We are such close friends here that I felt I could not keep my happiness to myself any longer."

Lady Atwood added her felicitations, and Phoebe, her appetite now completely gone, miserably pushed the food about her plate. Whatever had possessed Celeste to do such a thing? The Atwoods would be sure to spread the news when they returned to London, and if they did so, it would become more awkward to break the betrothal off. What must Mr. Huntsford think? Phoebe glanced at him, but he did not appear in the least upset—amused, if anything. Lord Murray had recovered and was receiving Lady Atwood's felicitations with equanimity. Only Olivia appeared as upset as she herself was.

Phoebe planned to corner Celeste directly when supper was over and ask why she had essentially announced her engagement to Lord Murray, but was thwarted in her plans by Lady Atwood. The lady had been much surprised by the news of the engagement and wished to question her about it. By the time Phoebe managed to escape, Celeste had disappeared.

CELESTE WALKED QUIETLY about the garden with Miles Huntsford, feeling very pleased with herself. The announcement she had made at dinner had certainly put a spoke in Olivia's wheel. The cat could not now pursue Lord Murray quite as blatantly as she had been. Although Olivia must have heard rumours of the betrothal, she had been behaving as though she was unaware of it. Now she could not. Mr. Huntsford's voice interrupted her satisfied thoughts.

"I know you were endeavouring to put the Honourable Miss Atwood in her place," he said lightly, "but was it wise?"

"I only stated the truth," Celeste said mischievously, not pretending to misunderstand.

"Is it indeed?" he queried, coming to a stop and regarding her seriously.

"Yes."

"To the letter, but not the fact, perhaps. However, I still think it was an ill-considered action. You did not think of the potential effects—on others as well as yourself. You should not have let girlish rivalries put you into a false position."

"I know what I am doing," Celeste said irritably, walking on. She did not care to have Mr. Huntsford remonstrate with her. Girlish rivalries, indeed! What did he know of the snubs and hurts Olivia had dealt both her and Phoebe over the past two years?

"My announcement will affect no one but Olivia, and she deserves a good set-down," she said shortly.

"You think not?" Miles said mildly. "Then I suggest that you have been so absorbed in your own concerns that you have not been aware of what was going on about you."

Celeste did not care to discuss the matter further and changed the subject. They strolled deeper into the garden and came to a stone bench, where they sat down. Miles seemed to have dismissed the topic of the supper from his mind, and they sat together several minutes in mutual enjoyment of the rare warm Scottish evening. Celeste dared to smile at him and he smiled back. How handsome he was in his claret-coloured evening coat! Not as romantic as he looked in his kilt, but very fine, nonetheless. She felt a sudden desire to have him kiss her, and fluttered her long black eyelashes over her green eyes, knowing from experience the likely effect on a man.

"Minx!" he said, flicking her cheek lightly with his fingertips. "But it will not serve to play your tricks upon me. Even I cannot be so much the cad as to kiss my cousin's acknowledged fiancée."

Celeste opened her eyes and her red lips pouted. "What made you think I wished you to kiss me? I desire no such thing. Your conceit makes you imagine things."

"You know very well you wished me to kiss you."

"I most certainly did not," Celeste retorted petulantly, tossing her head.

Miles Huntsford's indulgent amusement vanished. "Don't act like a child, my dear. You are getting to be of an age where such behaviour is not becoming. You cannot have both Robert and myself. It is not the thing to play fast and loose with a person's feelings, and that is what you are doing, and not only with us."

Celeste flushed with anger and mortification at the dressing down she was receiving. She was not accustomed to being reprimanded, and never so openly.

"It is not your place to object to my behaviour."

Miles studied Celeste a moment and then stood up. "Tell me when you are ready to grow up, my dear. Until then, I bid you good-night."

He turned and walked away, leaving Celeste alone in the darkening garden, near tears. She knew in her heart the reprimand had been deserved, but she could not bring herself to acknowledge that to Mr. Huntsford. For the same reason, she knew she would not tell Phoebe about the quarrel. How mortifying it would be to repeat Miles's words to her older, more experienced friend. Well, she thought angrily, she did not want Miles Huntsford, anyway. She was betrothed to Lord Murray, who was older, richer and of higher rank. She sniffed, banishing her tears, and was soon composed enough to return to the castle and join the others in the drawing room.

PHOEBE DID NOT get her opportunity to question Celeste while they were in the drawing room, but was confident she would when they retired. She prepared for bed and waited several minutes for Celeste to come in for their nightly coze, but she did not come. Phoebe finally tapped on the connecting door and went into Celeste's room. Celeste was standing before her glass, experimenting with ways to fix her hair, evidently oblivious to the havoc she had created that evening.

"Whatever possessed you to make your betrothal to Lord Murray public?" Phoebe said without preamble, irritated by her friend's apparent unconcern. "I know you want to make Olivia lose hope and leave, but that was not the way. Your betrothal will be much more difficult for you to end now."

Another scolding seemed too much to Celeste, especially from the friend who had always supported and understood her, even when no one else did.

"I *am* betrothed to Lord Murray, should you forget," she said rather truculently, turning to face Phoebe.

"But I thought you had realized you had made a mistake—that you were coming to care for Mr. Huntsford," Phoebe said, surprised and bewildered by Celeste's anger.

"Why ever would you think that?"

"Because you told me," Phoebe replied, puzzled. Celeste's antagonism was out of proportion to the severity of her scold.

"Well, I found I was mistaken. I wish to remain betrothed to Lord Murray," Celeste said shortly.

"But—"

"Why do you press me so," Celeste interrupted. She flung herself into the chair at the foot of her bed and scowled sullenly at her friend.

Phoebe was shocked by Celeste's anger and hurt by her refusal to confide in her.

"I am sorry to have disturbed you," she said stiffly and left the room, tears stinging her eyes.

When she had closed the door, Celeste threw herself across her bed and wept uncontrollably. She had lost the respect of the two people she loved most in the world after her mother and father.

HUNTSFORD AND ATWOOD finally voiced their intention to retire and Lord Murray thankfully made his way to his bedchamber. He was still feeling dazed by the abrupt turn of events. Whatever had possessed Miss Laurence to announce their betrothal to the Atwoods? He knew, of course, that it was somehow connected to the rivalry he had sensed between her and Miss Atwood, but what a foolish start!

He went into his chambers, and his valet, Dunbar, had just begun to remove his coat when a footman delivered a message from his aunt requesting that he join her in her room. Dunbar smoothed the coat back over his shoulders and he went to do his aunt's bidding.

Lady Melville was ensconced in a dainty damask-covered chair before her small chamber fireplace. She dismissed her maid when Lord Murray entered and motioned him to sit in the chair across from hers.

"I asked you to come to me here that we might speak privately," she said. "Now, what led to Miss Laurence's revelations at dinner? I had rather thought the two of you were coming to agree you should not suit."

"I had thought we were, too, Aunt," he said, a trace of bitterness in his voice. "But if Miss Laurence has changed her mind I shall be honour-bound to marry her."

"Of course," Lady Melville replied matter-of-factly, but her eyes conveyed her sympathy for his predicament.

"That was not the only thing of which I wished to speak," Lady Melville said after a few moments. "I have remarked that Dinsmore has been playing the pipes outside Miss Atwood's chamber every morning, and that she has been given a plate of oatmeal brose at every meal. That is according to her wishes?"

"Miss Atwood has often expressed her liking for oatmeal and pipe music," Lord Murray answered carefully. He, too, had noticed the routine and had made a good guess as to what the intended outcome was to be, but had chosen not to interfere. Frankly, he found it rather diverting to see Miss Atwood forced to back up her claims. As long as the joke went no further, he did not think any harm would come of it. But he did wonder with whom the idea had originated. Dinsmore, perhaps?

Her biggest concerns answered, Lady Melville addressed some minor problems that had arisen, and Lord Murray returned to his chamber. So even his aunt knew Miss Laurence was not the right wife for him, he thought as Dunbar again removed his coat. It appeared everyone was aware of their unsuitability except the girl herself.

ALTHOUGH SHE COULD NOT have thought it possible, Phoebe became even more miserable as the week progressed. Celeste continued to behave as though her betrothal to Lord Murray and eventual marriage to him was a foregone conclusion. Olivia was somewhat subdued, but she continued to follow her strategy of admiring all things Scottish, her enthusiasm making Phoebe wish she would choke on her oats. Lord Murray was more and more distant in his behaviour towards Phoebe. She could not help being hurt, but she realized that if Celeste persisted in going ahead with the betrothal, Lord Murray would have no choice but to marry her. Phoebe had tried again and again to persuade Celeste to confide in her, but was always rebuffed. This was the first time in their lives they had had a serious quarrel and she felt the estrangement keenly. The only person who remained the same was Wilfred, and consequently Phoebe sought to spend more time in his company.

She and Wilfred were on their way out one morning when they were stopped by Dinsmore.

"Miss Hartwell, there is to be another dance in the Great Hall this evening, and I thought perhaps Miss Atwood would like to attend, given her love of the pipes. And you also, Mr. Atwood."

"That is an excellent idea, Mr. Dinsmore," Phoebe agreed, thinking by the look in his eyes that Dinsmore must have something in mind.

"A dance? I'd like to attend, and Livvy is mad for Scottish customs," Wilfred agreed.

"A guest's likings maun be indulged," Dinsmore said blandly, and left.

"I know Livvy's enthusiasms must be wearing on you," Wilfred said to Phoebe as they continued on their way. "But you know how she is. Never gives up. She still wants Lord Murray, despite his betrothal to Miss Laurence."

"I do not think she is going to succeed," Phoebe said.

"No. I don't suppose she will. Thought at first he had taken my advice and you were the one Lord Murray had offered for," Wilfred added.

"You advised Lord Murray to offer for me?" Phoebe asked, not sure whether to feel amused or mortified.

"Oh, yes, and if he had would have spared himself all this."

Phoebe could not follow Wilfred's last reasoning, but his information was interesting. If Wilfred had advised Lord Murray to offer for her, he must have been considering her as well as Celeste, and for some reason chosen the younger girl instead. She wondered why.

THAT EVENING Lord Murray and his guests collected in the drawing room before going down to the dance. Lady Atwood was remaining upstairs with Lady Melville, but everyone else planned to attend. Olivia entered the room last, wearing a new white silk gown trimmed with bands of tartan. Phoebe had to admit Olivia looked very attractive, particularly with the matching tartan ribands wound through her dark hair. Phoebe felt she and Celeste looked very young next to Olivia, although Celeste outshone Olivia in sheer beauty.

Phoebe hardly dared glance at Lord Murray, lest her admiration of his appearance show too clearly, so she turned her attention to Mr. Huntsford instead. He was once again attired in full Highland dress, and Phoebe looked at Celeste to gage her reaction. But Celeste was studiously ignoring Mr. Huntsford, and Phoebe wondered if they had had a quarrel. They must have, she realized. That would explain much of Celeste's behaviour of late. What a pity she had been so immersed in her own troubles she had not noticed before.

Now that they were all assembled, Lord Murray led them downstairs. This time Lord Murray joined in the dancing, since Miles Huntsford and Wilfred were there to stay with Celeste if she did not wish to dance. He danced with Olivia first, patiently teaching her the steps and treating her gently. Phoebe watched with envy and Olivia intercepted the look, throwing her one of triumph.

Phoebe did not remain by the sidelines, however, for Mr. Huntsford asked her to dance. She hoped Lord Murray would request her hand for the next dance, but he did not, and Wilfred stepped in to fill the breech. He had just returned her to their group when two of Lord Murray's kinsmen approached. One of them asked Phoebe's hand for the dance and the other requested Olivia's. Phoebe saw Olivia's expression when the rough-looking Scotsman asked her to dance and she realized what Dinsmore had had in mind when he proffered his invitation. Despite her efforts, Olivia had not been able to conceal her disapproval of the Scots' more democratic ways, and nowhere did the Scottish gentleman feel more equal to everyone present than at one of their dances.

But however reluctant Olivia was to accept the kinsman's invitation, she dared not refuse and destroy the pose she had so carefully cultivated since her arrival. The four joined those already on the floor, and the reel commenced. As Phoebe was whirled about she tried to watch Olivia and her partner as well. To her great delight, Olivia's partner did not treat her gently as Lord Murray had, but swung her clear off the floor. Phoebe's own feet left the ground shortly thereafter and she could no longer watch Olivia. But when the reel ended and they were returned to their party, Phoebe could tell by Olivia's brittle voice as she thanked her partner that her sense of dignity had been outraged.

Not long after, Olivia pleaded a headache and excused herself to return upstairs. Celeste chose to accompany her, and Lord Murray was once again forced by good manners to leave the dance early, although Phoebe, Miles and Wilfred chose to remain. As Olivia went upstairs, Dinsmore caught Phoebe's eye and winked.

PHOEBE, tired from the exertion of the many reels she had danced, fell asleep almost immediately upon sinking into her bed that night. But later, she struggled to wake from her deep sleep, something telling her there was a reason to come fully awake. She managed to sit up and shook her head, trying to clear the clouds of sleep, and it was then she heard the sounds that must have awakened her. Muffled sobs were coming from Celeste's room. Knowing something must be very wrong, Phoebe got out of bed and softly entered Celeste's room.

Celeste lay with her head buried in her pillow, sobbing miserably. Forgetting their falling-out, Phoebe immediately went to her friend and gathered her into her arms, holding her close.

"Can you not tell me what is wrong, Celeste? Please do not keep it to yourself, whatever it is," she begged, smoothing the wet curls from Celeste's face.

Celeste made no answer and only sobbed harder. Phoebe, remembering her earlier suspicion, asked, "Have you quarrelled with Mr. Huntsford? Is that what is amiss?"

Celeste's sobs increased still more, but she managed to answer.

"Yes. He thinks I am nothing more than a spoiled child, and wants nothing more to do with me."

Slowly, between big gulping sobs, Celeste told Phoebe the whole story.

"Oh, Celeste," Phoebe said, still holding her close, "why *did* you announce your betrothal to

Lord Murray if you had already confessed your feelings to Miles Huntsford? Was it just to warn Olivia away?''

"Even you do not understand," Celeste said, sitting up in her bed, her tears beginning to abate. "I cannot bear to see Olivia be the one to marry Lord Murray. Remember how she has treated us in London—as though we were little better than kitchen maids, just because we do not have the word 'Honourable' or something grander before our names. I only intended to stay betrothed to Lord Murray until she left."

Phoebe felt she could understand Celeste's reason, much as she did not approve. Olivia's snubs must have cut the younger girl more deeply than she had realized.

"Was it fair to Lord Murray, though?" she asked mildly.

"Oh, he does not care deeply for me any more than I care for him," Celeste replied with conviction.

Phoebe felt the time had come for her to confide her own feelings. "But others did not know that, and were hurt by your impulsive behaviour. I, for one."

Her words stopped Celeste's tears entirely.

"You mean you care for Lord Murray? Miles said that I had been blind, but I could not credit it. Now I see that he knew you had formed a tendre for Lord Murray and I had no idea."

"Yes, I have," Phoebe admitted, thinking that Miles Huntsford was quite as keen an observer of people as she had suspected.

"Why ever did you not tell me?" Celeste exclaimed. "I am your *friend*."

"How could I tell you? You were betrothed to Lord Murray. I felt ashamed of my feelings for him, because I felt as if I were betraying you. At first I was not certain that you did not care for him, and then when it appeared that you did not, I had hoped to be able to talk to you privately and sort the matter out between us. Olivia arrived soon after that, and you know what happened. But, Celeste, my dear, I did so try to talk to you, the night you acknowledged your betrothal to Lord Murray, but you refused to listen."

"I am sorry. If I had known how important it was for you to speak to me, I would have listened. But I was so hurt and shamed by my quarrel with Mr. Huntsford that I could not bring myself to talk to anyone. Oh, Phoebe, I've been such a fool. I truly do love Mr. Huntsford."

They hugged each other tightly, glad to be friends once more.

"You must go to Mr. Huntsford and tell him exactly what you have told me," Phoebe advised her young friend. "I feel sure he will forgive you. He is only waiting for you to approach him and admit your mistake."

"Yes, I will, but I shall first have to break off with Lord Murray. Oh, dear," Celeste said in distress, "but if I were to end my betrothal to Lord Murray right away, Olivia will stay and pursue him more determinedly than ever. What about you and Lord Murray?"

"I shouldn't worry, I shall simply have to take my chances," Phoebe responded. "You cannot allow this misunderstanding to continue. Besides, I do not think Lord Murray can be persuaded to marry Olivia if he does not wish to do so. We must enjoy her company as best we may. None of our plans to make her leave have worked. Perhaps," Phoebe laughed, "you should use some of your faery-power to encourage her swift departure."

When Celeste had become aware that everyone in the castle were convinced she had been sent by the Daoine Shi', she had been more flattered than offended by the Highlanders' notion she was connected with the faery folk. Privately, she thought it quite a compliment.

"Perhaps I shall," she agreed, laughing with Phoebe.

Both feeling better than they had since their falling-out, the friends went back to bed and slept soundly through the rest of the night.

CHAPTER ELEVEN

CELESTE, GIVEN HOPE and courage by Phoebe's words, decided to take her advice and speak to Miles Huntsford. First though, she had to end her betrothal to Lord Murray. Wishing to get the deed over with as soon as possible, she sought him out in his study the morning following her talk with Phoebe.

Lord Murray's dark head was bent over some papers he was apparently much absorbed in, for he did not hear Celeste's light step as she entered the room. She paused for a moment, contemplating the man whose suit she had accepted. She could not regret her action, for it had led to her meeting Miles, but she understood now that *had* she gone through with the marriage, love was not something that would have come afterward. Not true romantic love. That was something one felt immediately, in one's heart, as she had for Miles. She wondered if Phoebe felt the same way for Lord Murray. She did not see how she could, for Lord Murray had none of the urbanity Miles did, but perhaps different qualities engendered feelings of love in different people.

"Lord Murray, may I speak to you?" she asked, stepping forward.

He looked up with a welcoming smile. "Of course, Miss Laurence. Please sit down," he added as he stood to draw a chair near his desk.

Celeste went directly to the point.

"Lord Murray, I have come to the conclusion that we should not suit," she said baldly.

"I rather suspected you would arrive at that decision," Lord Murray said, relieved that she had recovered her senses in time. Over the past few days he had feared she would not. "I agree that we should not be a good match, although you will always remain high in my esteem."

He paused, and then added, "Since our betrothal was never officially announced, I see no reason to inform anyone of our change of mind beyond our immediate families."

Celeste heard Lord Murray's latter words with great relief. Perhaps the Atwoods need not learn of the broken engagement. If they did not, Olivia would have no reason to linger.

"I hope this will not cause you and Miss Hartwell to shorten your stay," he continued. "I would be pleased to have you both as my guests for as long as you wish."

"Thank you, Lord Murray. Our visit has been most delightful and we should be glad to remain awhile longer," Celeste accepted on behalf of herself and Phoebe. In truth, Celeste was not eager to leave Miles just yet and more time would also allow Phoebe that opportunity to become more familiar with Lord Murray now that they would not have the constraint of the betrothal between them. She smiled sunnily. Everything was going to come right in the end.

Directly after her successful interview with Lord Murray, Celeste went in search of Miles Huntsford. She was not as confident as to the result of this meeting. Phoebe had assured her Miles was only waiting for her to speak first, but what if she was wrong? He had shown no signs of relenting, and only spoke to her when courtesy demanded it. She felt her heart begin to beat fast and her hands become moist with nervousness as she tried to compose a suitable apology.

Celeste could not find Miles, and discovered he was out riding with Wilfred. The enforced wait increased her anxiety, and by the time he returned, her nerves were in a pitiable state. She heard him coming up the stairway with Wilfred, and waited at the top.

"Mr. Huntsford, might I speak to you privately?" she asked.

Miles did not appear to be surprised by her request. He excused himself from Wilfred and led her to the library. He bade her to be seated, and sat himself, but Celeste sprang up again almost immediately. She was too discomposed to sit still. Now that the moment was upon her, she was afraid to speak. What if he would not forgive her? She made a couple of quick turns about the room, and then came to stand stiffly before Miles' chair.

"I want to ask your forgiveness for my behaviour this past sennight," she said, embarking upon her prepared words. "You were correct, I was behaving like a child. I *was* playing fast and loose with other people's feelings with no thought for the hurt I might cause them. I spoke to Lord Murray this morning, and we have agreed we should not suit."

After coming this far in her rehearsed speech, she faltered and suddenly the words were just pouring out, "It was only that I could not bear to see Olivia marry Lord Murray, and I thought he would end up in her clutches if I broke off the engagement during her visit. She has been so unkind to me and Phoebe, you cannot imagine! I could not let her win for she would have bruited about her victory and Society would have been all atwitter over the match of the Season. I could not allow her to marry the only eligible Highland lord."

Miles Huntsford laughed as he watched Celeste turn from a carefully controlled young lady to an irrepressible and angry child once more. At six-and-twenty he was not so far beyond his own youth that he did not recall how painful it was to feel outside the exclusive circle of society or to suffer unkind treatment that was considered unjust and undeserved.

"I do not think you need worry about Robert marrying Miss Atwood," he said reassuringly. "He has his own mind. Come here," he commanded, when finally she had the courage to look at him.

Celeste collected her composure and went to stand directly before him. He reached out suddenly and pulled her into his lap. Before she could recover from her surprise, he had bent his head over her face and began kissing her expertly. Celeste had never been kissed in such a fashion before, and found she quite liked it. She felt disappointed when he stopped, and looked at him questioningly. He smiled tenderly and playfully tugged her black curls.

"As for making the Match of the Season, my cousin is not the only Scotsman in the world. You shall marry me and astound Society."

"I shall?" Celeste challenged, thinking to disagree since he had ordered her and had not asked, but the expression in his eyes prompted her to change her mind. "I shall," she agreed mildly, and the next several minutes were spent in a most delightfully satisfactory manner.

CELESTE'S NEWS overjoyed Phoebe, and she hoped that now Lord Murray might feel free to admit his interest in her, but days passed without her hopes being realized. Had his feelings changed? Or was it perhaps because the Atwoods were still under the impression that he and Celeste were engaged and he was reluctant to give any rise to suspicion? They had all arrived at a tacit agreement not to inform the Atwoods of either the end of Celeste's betrothal to Lord

Murray or her new betrothal to Mr. Huntsford. Although how anyone could be unaware of the latter Phoebe did not know, given the besotted looks Celeste and Mr. Huntsford could not help exchanging. Certainly the Atwoods showed no signs of planning to depart, she thought, glancing at Olivia and her mother where they sat under the drawing-room window.

Phoebe sighed and picked up her fancywork. The days seemed to have become excessively tedious, she thought. It was dull to sit about the castle all day, but Olivia's presence invariably cancelled out any livelier occupations such as walking or riding.

She felt a touch on her arm and turned to find Celeste regarding her with some concern. Celeste was clad in a pale green muslin day frock, and her inner happiness had given her such a glow that she seemed to have become more beautiful than ever. Phoebe suddenly felt old and tired next to her younger friend and sighed once more.

"Are you not feeling quite the thing, Miss Hartwell?" Olivia asked, responding to Phoebe's second sigh. "You look quite peaked."

Miles Huntsford had entered the drawing room in time to overhear Olivia's remarks. "Perhaps you would care to go for a walk, Miss Hartwell?" he suggested. "The fresh air would do you a world of good."

"What an excellent idea. We shall all join you," Olivia said, rising.

Celeste and Phoebe exchanged a look of disgust and resignation, but there was nothing for it but to go. Wilfred went to recruit Lord Murray's presence, and a short time later the party set out on a path across the meadows to the southwest of the castle.

Olivia, as usual, managed to walk beside Lord Murray. She was not accustomed to long distances, and before many minutes had passed, called a halt so she could rest. Phoebe and Celeste went to gather some wildflowers, and Olivia went to stand upon a grassy knoll, knowing she would appear to advantage there silhouetted against the pale grey-blue sky.

"Careful, Miss Atwood," Miles Huntsford said teasingly, "you have stopped upon a faery spot. You would not wish to call the faeries' attention to you this morning. You are clad in green, and they might take it amiss."

Olivia looked down in puzzlement at her fashionable green pelisse with yellow fringe.

"The faeries consider green to be their colour, Miss Atwood," Lord Murray explained. "They do not like mortals to wear it without their permission."

Olivia hesitated, not quite sure how to respond. Mr. Huntsford might only be quizzing her though she very much doubted Lord Murray would. Faeries had also been mentioned in *Lady of the Lake,* and if the Scots believed them to exist she was reluctant to say anything that would tarnish her perfect performance. However, she did not care to be singled out and felt obliged to defend herself.

"But Miss Laurence is also wearing green," she said, gesturing towards Celeste. "And your tartan has green," she added to Mr. Huntsford.

"Ah, but the Murrays have the faeries' permission, and as for Miss Laurence, she is another matter. She was sent by the faeries."

"Yes," said Celeste mischievously, "and I must warn you you are standing on the roof of one of their houses. They live underground beneath these hummocks."

"Best move, Livvy," Wilfred advised. "They might take offence if you stand on their roof."

"Oh, I am sure they will forgive me since I am in company with one of their own," she said lightly, indicating Celeste. To show she did not fear their displeasure, she did not move away, but sat upon the hummock to rest. "It's too ridiculous to believe in faeries," she muttered under her breath. In truth she found most Highland customs ridiculous.

THAT EVENING AT SUPPER Phoebe wondered if they would ever be rid of Olivia's company or if she and Celeste would have to admit defeat and leave first. Certainly none of their plans had succeeded. Not the oats, the pipes, or even Dinsmore's idea of the dance. As she helped herself to a venison pastry, she saw the servant bring Olivia her usual plate of brose and reflected that one really had to give Olivia credit. Much as Phoebe herself liked oatmeal she doubted she could have tolerated eating a bowl of brose every meal for such a long time.

Wilfred was also watching his sister eat the porridge and shook his head in wonderment.

"Must say, Livvy, you've taken an extraordinary liking to oats. Have to find out how to prepare them and give the receipts to our cook in London."

"What a good idea," Olivia agreed, although the look she shot her brother belied the veracity of her words.

"Hand me the preserved fruit, will you Livvy," Wilfred added to his sister.

Olivia reached across her plate and picked up the green glass jar of preserved apricots and began to pass it to her brother. Phoebe, who was seated across from her, saw the jar suddenly slip from Olivia's grasp and fall into her plate of brose, splashing the sticky mixture all over her pretty silk gown. Everyone had looked round at the noise, and then had hastily averted their eyes. Olivia fought desperately to keep her composure.

"If you will excuse me," she murmured, rising. A servant came forward to clear her place, and noticing a large clot of the brose sticking to Olivia's hair, attempted to remove it. Olivia batted the servant away and was turning to leave the room when she caught sight of herself in the glass on the wall. She froze. Oatmeal clumps spotted her gown liberally, creating water stains that were spreading rapidly across the silk. Smaller pieces were spattered on her neck and face, and a particularly offensive lump was dripping slowly down her décolletage.

A snigger he was unable to smother escaped Wilfred, and the sound seemed to instantly release Olivia from her deep freeze. With a suddenness and ferocity that stunned the whole table, she exploded in anger.

"Oats!" she screamed. "I loathe them! No wonder in England we give them to our horses. They are not fit food for people.

"In fact," she continued, turning to address the assembled company, "I detest everything Scottish—oats, bagpipes, tartan, faeries and presumptuous servants and poor relations who won't know their place. Mr. Scott must have been out of his senses to write a poem in praise of such a barbarous country with nothing at all to recommend it to civilized people."

Her tirade stopped as suddenly as it had begun, and with a strangled cry she rushed from the room.

For a moment everyone sat in shocked silence. A sense of deep shame invaded Phoebe. She knew that she was mostly at fault and remonstrated with herself for her lack of sensibilities. Olivia would never have lost her composure and made such a scene if Phoebe had not carried the matter so far. She could not be proud of herself even though victory seemed assured.

Lord Murray was the first to recover himself. He turned to Lady Atwood with a commonplace remark, as if the scene that had just transpired had never occurred. The others followed his lead, and some semblance of normal conversation resumed, although all appeared to have lost their appetite.

When Lady Melville stood to signal the ladies to retire to the drawing room, Phoebe took the opportunity to slip upstairs and look in on Olivia. Phoebe had not changed her opinion of Olivia. She could never be considered a pleasant person, but Phoebe was feeling very remorseful and thought that a little sympathy would not be amiss. With some trepidation she tapped at Olivia's door and entered.

Every trace of oatmeal had disappeared from Olivia's person, and her maid was fastening the ties of a clean gown on her mistress.

"Is there anything I can do?" Phoebe asked inadequately, hesitating just inside the door.

Olivia turned to Phoebe, anger written all over her face. "You have done quite enough, thank you," she replied. "You think I do not know who is responsible for all the oats I have been served, and the pipe music played at my door? Scottish hospitality, indeed! I have also noticed how you dote on Lady Melville and give orders to the housekeeper and butler as if you were in your own home. Do you think to be the mistress of this castle? Do you hope that now Celeste has rejected Lord Murray, that he will marry you? I can assure you that the only reason he would do so would be out of pity and admiration for your housekeeping skills.''

Phoebe looked surprised, thinking Olivia must have heard of Celeste's ended engagement. Olivia interpreted her expression accurately.

''Yes, I have heard of the end of her betrothal to Lord Murray,'' she said scornfully. ''Did you think to keep it a secret? The servants always hear everything.''

Her maid had finished tying the ribands of the frock, and Olivia went to stand directly before Phoebe where she still stood just inside the door.

''I have tried my best to befriend you and Miss Laurence,'' she said, ''but you, especially, have always resented me because of my superior beauty and ties to the aristocracy. I shall befriend you no longer, and you will come to regret what you have done. When you return to London there will be no more invitations to even the smallest of the entertainments held by the ton. And you *shall* return to London. If you think Lord Murray will offer for you when I am gone you will find you are very much mistaken.''

Olivia paused and deliberately surveyed Phoebe from head to toe. ''You.'' She laughed contemptuously. ''You do not even have the saving graces of beauty and wealth, or a noble grandfather, as Miss Laurence does. What a fool you are. Now, get out! And never cross my path again!''

Olivia's last words were spoken with such venom that Phoebe involuntarily stepped backwards, and then turned and left the room without a word. She had been silent during the whole tirade, thinking that she had deserved the set-down, in part, at least. But Olivia's final accusations were entirely without foundation. Olivia had been the one to pursue their "friendship," not she and Celeste. Nor had she ever resented Olivia. She could easily dismiss Olivia's opinions regarding her chances of becoming Lord Murray's wife, but she could not dismiss the lingering feeling that she had broken the Scots' code of hospitality towards their guests. Worse, if Olivia departed, as she had indicated that she would, the responsibility for inhospitality would fall to Lord Murray, since it was his home. She had inadvertently placed him in an untenable position. What must *he* think of her?

As Phoebe made her way towards the drawing room, she passed a frosty Lady Atwood who was obviously intent upon seeking out her daughter. Phoebe found the company gathered in the drawing room very subdued. Wilfred looked even more rumpled than usual, which caused Phoebe to feel that much worse. Wilfred would be obliged to accompany his sister and mother back to London, and he had always been a good friend. He seemed to sense her eyes upon him and looked up. For a moment Phoebe hesitated, but as he rose, she crossed the room so they could speak.

"Daresay Livvy must want to leave now," he said.

"Yes, and I want to confess that her desire to do so is partly my fault," Phoebe said remorsefully. "I was the one who told Mrs. Baird and Dinsmore how she liked oatmeal brose and pipe music."

"She *did* say she liked those things," Wilfred responded matter-of-factly. "Livvy brought this all on herself. *I* don't blame you. I expect you don't think I noticed, but I know how she treated you in London, using your acquaintance to puff up her consequence. Tit for tat. Maybe she's even learned a lesson, but I doubt it," he finished.

Phoebe still looked miserable, and Wilfred patted her hand reassuringly. She smiled gratefully and allowed him to lead her to a chair in the corner of the room. She was glad Wilfred did not hold the incident against her, for she would have been extremely sorry to lose his friendship.

LORD MURRAY WATCHED WILFRED pat Phoebe's hand and draw her to the corner chairs. His grave face took on an even more solemn expression. What a disaster this evening had been! He had been painfully embarrassed for Olivia as well as for her mother and brother. He also felt he was partly to blame for not calling a halt to the lark. Now Lady Atwood and Olivia would leave in high dudgeon, and Miss Hartwell and Miss Laurence would be forced to follow suit. Worse, what would Lord Atwood think of him now? And after the welcome he had been given at the baron's home!

Lady Melville left the drawing room, presumably to seek out Lady Atwood in an effort to smooth things over, and Miss Hartwell and Miss Laurence retired to their chambers soon after, leaving the three gentlemen alone in the drawing room. Lord Murray took advantage of their relative privacy to apologize to Wilfred.

"You are not to blame," Wilfred assured Lord Murray. "It was Olivia's own doing, and so I'll tell her. Just clumsy of her to drop the preserve dish—no one to blame. Odd, that—it just seemed to slip from her grasp as if it were greased."

Lord Murray was greatly relieved by Wilfred's generous attitude and pressed him to return to Castle Abermaise anytime, an invitation Wilfred accepted with alacrity.

"Like to try the sport here in the fall," he confessed, "and know m'father would, too. Say, maybe Phoebe would come as well. That would make a jolly party."

Wilfred's reference to Miss Hartwell only served to reinforce the conclusion Lord Murray had not been able to avoid. It appeared as if Miss Hartwell had decided against his own offer and had instead chosen to remain betrothed to Atwood. If she ever did return to Castle Abermaise, she would do so as the wife of another man.

THE ATWOODS DEPARTED early the next morning. After they had left, Phoebe screwed up her courage and asked to speak to Lord Murray privately. Surprised by her request, he led her to his study.

"Lord Murray, I wish to apologize for driving your guests away," she began, and confessed that she had been behind the pranks from the start. "I have informed Lady Atwood of my culpability," she finished. "I did not wish you to be blamed for my misguided actions."

"Thank you, Miss Hartwell, for your generous concern, but I hold myself equally responsible, if not entirely so," he replied gravely. "I was quite aware of the goings-on and did nothing to alter the course of events. If you wish to apportion blame," he added wryly, "I suspect some should also be attached to Mrs. Baird, Balneaves and Dinsmore."

Then, noting the increase in Phoebe's distress, he said firmly, "Let us speak no more of the matter, Miss Hartwell. If you insist on sharing the burden of guilt, let me assure you I wholeheartedly forgive you your part."

Phoebe smiled weakly at Lord Murray and took her leave, but she had rather he had raked her over the coals as she had deserved than coldly dismissed her without so much as a smile.

PHOEBE HAD EXPECTED that as a result of the Atwoods' departure, all at the castle would revert to its former pleasantness, but it was not so. Or rather not for herself, she amended. Celeste and Mr. Huntsford, at least, were content. She tried not to envy them their happiness, but at times it was difficult not to, for it seemed more certain than ever that Lord Murray no longer considered her much more than a guest. He had not made any attempt to reestablish their former closeness. Had she not treasured the kiss by the lake, she might have been persuaded it had never been. She remembered he had said that day that when his betrothal ended he would kiss her again. And so it had, but he had hardly spoken to her, much less kissed her. The Atwoods were no longer in residence, so their presence had not been the reason for his continuing circumspection. Phoebe feared that despite his words to the contrary, Lord Murray had not forgiven her for causing the departure of his guests. Or perhaps, she thought suddenly, Olivia had been correct. Perhaps it *was* her lack of wealth. It could not be her inferior status or her father's profession as a barrister—he had already known of those facts. But perhaps he had not known how poor she was until one of the Atwoods had informed him. Olivia would have been more than happy to disclose that information.

Celeste was not so lost in her own happiness that she had not noticed something was amiss with her friend.

"What is it that makes you so downcast?" she asked one evening as Sara helped Phoebe disrobe.

"Hasn't Lord Murray given any indication of wanting to offer for you yet?"

"No, and I do not think he will," Phoebe replied sadly. "He hardly speaks to me at all.

"Celeste, we cannot stay here much longer," she said to her friend as she took a seat so Sara could give her bright curls their nightly brushing. "Now that your betrothal to Lord Murray is at an end, we really have no reason to remain."

"But if we leave you will have no chance to attach Lord Murray's affections," Celeste objected, taking the hairbrush from Sara's hand and stroking Phoebe's red curls herself.

"I would not anyway. He will never forgive me," Phoebe said with uncharacteristic pessimism.

"I do not think you are right," Celeste contradicted. "It is not in Lord Murray's nature to hold a grudge—even I can see that. I shall talk to him for you."

"Do not dare," Phoebe warned, afraid her friend might do just that.

"You told me before *I* was acting foolish. Now you are the one," Celeste said, setting the brush down and moving to look directly at Phoebe. "If you do not talk to him, how can you be sure *what* he feels?"

"This is different," Phoebe asserted illogically. "Promise you will not talk to Lord Murray. Or Mr. Huntsford, either," she added, familiar with the way Celeste's mind worked.

"I promise," Celeste said reluctantly, knowing her friend was not going to be satisfied until she did. "But I still think you are being foolish."

"Perhaps," Phoebe acknowledged. "But whichever of us is correct, we still cannot stay here. We must leave soon."

"Let us stay a sennight longer," Celeste pleaded. "Miles says he will travel back with us then, as he must speak to Mama and Papa and explain the change in the person of my fiancé."

Celeste laughed at the thought of her parents' reaction to the turn of events, and even Phoebe managed a smile.

"*One* week," Phoebe agreed, not totally reluctant to be persuaded.

"You will be back together with Lord Murray before the week is out, you will see," Celeste promised, giving her friend an encouraging hug.

CHAPTER TWELVE

LORD MURRAY STRODE purposefully up the hill, oblivious to the chilly morning air and the stickers on the hawthorn bushes that tore angrily at his buckskins, his gillie close behind. He had hoped some vigorous exercise would help to disperse the depression of spirits that had settled upon him since the departure of the Atwoods, but it was not serving the trick. Whatever he did, thoughts of the red-haired Miss Hartwell and her imminent departure dominated his mind. The knowledge that she belonged to another, had *chosen* another over him, made no difference in his feelings for her, and did not help him banish her loveliness from his heart.

He reached the top of the hill and halted, standing on one of the large bare rock clearings that dotted the Highland hills. He folded his arms across his chest and stared moodily out over the loch and the rugged mountains encircling it. Pockets of mist amongst the trees and water made a patchwork of grey, green and blue, the morning sun trimming the whole with a fringe of gold. Previously such a view of his beloved Highlands had had the power to heal his spirit, but this time the unearthly beauty had al-

most the opposite effect. What was such magnific-
ence if one had no one to share it with?

Lord Murray sighed deeply. Much as he dreaded
her leaving, sometimes he could almost wish the day
of Miss Hartwell's departure were upon them. Perhaps after she left the pain he felt would lessen, although he doubted it. The worst part of all was that
there appeared to be nothing he could do to alter the
course of events. At times he thought of trying to
speak to Phoebe, to convince her he was much more
suited to make her happy than a callow hafling like
Atwood ever could. Other times he actually considered keeping her forcibly at Castle Abermaise and
tricking her into a Scottish marriage. Such thoughts
arose from his Highland ancestors, no doubt, ori-
ginating back in the times such deeds, and worse,
had been perpetrated. But, however tempted he
might have been to pursue such a course, he knew he
could not actually do so. If Phoebe would not come
to him of her own free will, he could not steal her
from Atwood. Particularly not after driving Miss
Atwood, and thereby Lady Atwood and Wilfred as
well, from his home. Such an action would be inex-
cusable, completely beyond the bounds of civilized
behaviour.

Thinking of the Atwoods reminded Lord Murray
that one of his worries, at least, had been removed.
The previous day he had received a packet containing two letters—one from Lord Atwood, cordial,
and it had been evident that the baron did not hold

him to blame for anything that had occurred to overset his wife and daughter. In fact, the baron had written that he and his son intended to visit Castle Abermaise the coming autumn to hunt the red deer, although no mention had been made of Lady Atwood and Olivia joining the party.

A smile briefly touched Lord Murray's lips as he recalled an amusing bit of news in the letter he had received from Wilfred. It appeared that Miss Atwood had become the new goddess of Mr. Arnold, and that she was encouraging his attentions. No doubt such total devotion as the excessively handsome Mr. Arnold could give was balm to her wounded ego and compensated for his lowly occupation of solicitor.

Restlessly, Lord Murray shifted his stance and sighed again. He wished his heart might be as easily mended as Miss Atwood's, but he knew that if he could not have Miss Hartwell he would never marry anyone. Let Balneaves and Mrs. Baird say what they might about a laird's duty to his people. He would make Miles his heir. Although, he thought wryly, Miss Laurence would probably not appreciate the gesture.

Lord Murray became aware that his gillie was staring fixedly at the sky, and followed the direction of his glance. The sun was indeed rising high, he thought, taking the silent hint. It was time he went back and tended to his business. He could not neglect all his duties because of his personal heartache. He must accustom himself to working despite the pain, for he doubted he would ever be free from it.

PHOEBE IGNORED the soft knock at the door of her bedchamber, turning her head into the pillow in case Celeste should peek in to see if she were awake. Perhaps it was cowardly, but she suspected Celeste might lecture her again about speaking frankly to Lord Murray, and she did not want to listen. The past week had been a difficult one, and she wanted to spend this day, her last full one at Castle Abermaise, by herself. She needed the time to fortify herself for the long journey home with Celeste and Miles, a journey that would take Celeste ever closer to her happiness, and Phoebe ever farther from hers.

For Celeste's prediction had not been fulfilled—Phoebe and Lord Murray were no nearer to cordial relations than they had been a sennight ago. His manner towards her had not changed at all the past week. He was unfailingly polite to her, but his courtesy was like an impenetrable wall, keeping her at a distance. Only twice when she had surprised him looking at her she thought she had discerned a flash of pain in his eyes, but that was the only emotion she had been able to detect. And even that, she admitted reluctantly, might have been wishful thinking on her part.

A tear escaped from Phoebe's eye and rolled wetly down her nose into the thick goosedown pillow. If only she could understand why things had altered so.

The more she thought on the matter, the more she was inclined to believe Olivia had been correct, lowering as the thought was, and that it was her lack of fortune that had caused Lord Murray to change his mind. As Celeste had said, Lord Murray did not seem the type to hold a grudge, and privately she agreed, but if Lord Murray required his wife to bring a sizable dowry into the marriage, that would explain a great deal.

In her heart, Phoebe longed to do as Celeste had advised and ask Lord Murray directly if it was her lack of fortune that was keeping him from her, but a combination of diffidence and fear kept her from doing so. Not only did she not want to put Lord Murray in the embarrassing position of having to admit he was in pressing need of money, but she also did not want to risk putting herself in the mortifying position of finding out the truth was something even worse. What if his distant behaviour was caused not by the fact that he could not afford to marry her, but because he had simply discovered he did not love her?

Phoebe heard a door close, and the sound of Celeste's light footsteps passed her door and faded down the hallway. Feeling safe for the moment, Phoebe slipped out of her bed and began dressing without ringing for her maid. This morning she did not want anyone's company.

As she completed her simple toilette, Phoebe looked about her room with a feeling of sadness.

Tomorrow she would leave. Never again would she see this grey-and-gold room with its elegant Chippendale furnishings. The time she had spent at Castle Abermaise would become like a dream. Phoebe pictured herself in the years to come, an aging apeleader living in the memories of what once was. Well, she thought, trying to give herself courage to face her bleak future, it would be better to have something to remember than never to have experienced anything at all of love. But still that was small compensation for the pain of losing her heart's desire.

The thought of her empty future gave Phoebe an idea of how to spend her last day. She would revisit all the places where she had been so happy, impressing their images indelibly upon her mind so she would be able to recall them in every detail for years to come. And the first place she would go would be to the spot above the lake where Lord Murray had kissed her.

Phoebe pulled a pelisse from her wardrobe, not thinking to take a hat. After checking to see that no one was in the passageway, she slipped out of her bedchamber and managed to step quickly and quietly past the door of the breakfast room without being seen by Celeste or anyone else. As she descended the stairway into the main hall, the sound of the pipes filled her ears, and she saw Dinsmore striding back and forth across the Hall, playing one of the mournful tunes he seemed to prefer of late. His eyes flickered over her as he marched past the stairway, and Phoebe smiled, but her smile was met with a stern look of disapprobation. Everyone seemed out of sorts with her of late, Phoebe thought dismally as she continued down the stairs.

As Phoebe crossed the Hall, the aroma of Mrs. Baird's delicious cooking wafted past her nose and a hollow feeling in her stomach reminded her she had not had any breakfast. Not being in the mood for company, Phoebe decided to ask Mrs. Baird for something she could take with her to eat on her walk, and she turned back towards the kitchen. As she approached the doorway, Phoebe could hear raised voices and smiled to herself. Balneaves and Mrs. Baird were arguing again.

"I tell you, only straight speaking will put things right at this point," Balneaves's voice said.

"Straight speaking willna dae a thing wi' two who be sae doure an' blin', ye Hieland limmer," Mrs. Baird retorted snappishly.

"Stubborn and blind they may be, but I—" Balneaves broke off as he became aware of Phoebe standing in the doorway.

"Good morning, Miss Hartwell. Is there anything you require?" he asked formally.

"I wished to ask Mrs. Baird if she had something I might take with me on my walk. I find that I am very hungry this morning," Phoebe replied, with an uncomfortable feeling that Balneaves, too, was displeased with her for some reason. Was everyone upset with her because of the Atwoods' precipitate departure?

"Och, aye," Mrs. Baird said, nodding. "Tak some o' my farls," she offered, holding a basket of thin oatcakes out to Phoebe, who took two and slipped them into the pocket of her pelisse.

Mrs. Baird's glance ran over Phoebe, resting a moment on her bare head. Suddenly she smiled and patted Phoebe's hand. "Lassie," she said in a warm voice, "I ken you hae been sair fashit o' late. You micht gae tae speir help o' the water-kelpies afore you gang awa."

"I did plan to go to the lake this morning," Phoebe admitted, hoping her low spirits were not as obvious to everyone as they evidently were to Mrs. Baird. "But I did not know that I could apply to the kelpies for their assistance, since unlike Celeste, I was not sent by the faeries."

"Ane niver kens what themsels micht dae an it taks their fancy," Mrs. Baird said. "But it canna hurt tae try."

"Perhaps I shall ask them for their help, then," Phoebe agreed with a smile, grateful that one person at least did not appear to be at outs with her. She thanked the housekeeper for the farls and made her escape from the castle, the gillie rising from his seat at the Hall table and following her as she left.

Phoebe walked slowly down the path to the lake, munching on the farls and noting every bush and flower, trying to impress them upon her memory.

The individual plants were about all she could make out, for a heavy mist roamed the landscape, its tendrils curling through the bushes and swirling about her feet. But she could still see enough to find the side path Lord Murray had shown her the day he took her to his special place, and her steps quickened as she began the climb. As the path became steeper and rockier, Phoebe heard the gillie close behind, ready to assist her if she should need it. It was a tiring climb, but at last Phoebe scrambled onto the large rock overhanging the lake. When she had seated herself securely, the gillie moved back to stand a discreet distance away. Phoebe waved her thanks to the imperturbable kinsman of Lord Murray and then turned her attention to the lake.

Never again would she look out over this beautiful view, Phoebe thought unhappily, and after the morrow never again would she see the castle, or Dinsmore, the gillie, Balneaves, Mrs. Baird, or Lord Murray. Scotland would become part of her past. For a few minutes Phoebe allowed herself to indulge in a fit of the dismals, and then she took herself severely to task. She was really becoming quite morbid, and it simply would not do. She might be losing Lord Murray, but she still had her family, Celeste and even Wilfred. Losing one person did not mean the end of all one's happiness. She must not forget to appreciate what she had.

A moist cool breeze blew in from over the lake, and Phoebe pulled her light summer pelisse more closely about her shoulders as she gazed at the water. How mysterious it appeared under the shifting blanket of morning mist. One moment she could see the surface clearly, and the next her view was obscured. The kelpies must be about, she thought, or the Daoine Shi'. On a morning like this such spirits seemed very real. One could almost see them. Perhaps she *should* ask them for their help, as Mrs. Baird had advised, Phoebe mused. If to do so could not help, it could not hurt, either.

She looked down into the dense blue water lapping softly at the rocky shore and whispered very quietly, "Help me, please, stay here where I belong." Under the eerie spell cast by the thick grey mist, Phoebe half-expected some kind of sign that they had heard her plea and felt ridiculously disappointed when there was no response but another wave of mist and the calls of the birds as they glided over the lake looking for a meal.

Phoebe sighed resignedly and stared into the distance. She had been sitting still several minutes, lost in her thoughts, when a rock clattered loudly in the muffled quiet. She turned her head, expecting to see the gillie, and gasped in surprise as her eyes lit upon Lord Murray standing a few yards away. Clad as he was in buckskins and a plaid, she might have mistaken him for a character straight out of *Lady of the Lake* had it not been for the woman's silk-lined straw bonnet dangling incongruously from his left hand.

"I'm sorry, Miss Hartwell, I did not mean to startle you," he said. "Mrs. Baird saw you walking this way without a head covering, and since she was worried lest you take sick from the morning cold, I thought to bring one to you."

Phoebe still said nothing, and Lord Murray began to feel very foolish. The excuse to follow Phoebe that had sounded so plausible at the time Mrs. Baird had confided her worry to him now seemed lame indeed. What must Phoebe be thinking of him, a man who would follow another's betrothed to such an isolated spot? Uncertainly he held the bonnet out to her.

"Thank you," Phoebe said, finding her voice. The shock of seeing Lord Murray so suddenly had momentarily deprived her of her senses. For a second she had actually wondered if the kelpies *had* conjured him up. She took the bonnet and laid it on the rock beside her, searching for the right words to say. Had he really come to bring her the hat, or was it possible he had used it as a pretext to come speak to her privately?

"I've disturbed you, so I'll take my leave," Lord Murray said, the feeling he was making a fool of himself causing him to clip his words.

"There is no need for you to leave, Lord Murray," Phoebe replied, chagrin at his manner making her voice equally cool. "It is your land, after all."

Another chill breeze blew in from the lake, rocking Phoebe's bonnet and causing her to pull her pelisse more tightly about her shoulders.

Lord Murray noted Phoebe's shiver and longed to warm her by taking her into his arms and holding her close, kissing her as he had before in this very place. He wondered if she remembered that time, too. Was it possible that was why she had come here? He looked hopefully into her eyes, searching for some sign she still cared for him a little, but their clear hazel revealed nothing.

Another, stronger, gust of wind blew, swirling about and abruptly changing its direction, blowing Phoebe's bonnet into the lake.

"Oh, dear!" Phoebe exclaimed. "And after you took such trouble to bring it to me," she cried, looking after the hat in dismay.

The first sign of emotion Phoebe showed, and it was over a straw bonnet! Exasperation further chilled the timbre of Lord Murray's voice.

"It is of no moment, Miss Hartwell. But do allow me to escort you back to the castle. The weather is chill and you are not dressed appropriately."

"You need not trouble yourself, Lord Murray. I am quite warm enough," Phoebe responded briefly, feeling frustrated and not a little angry at his impenetrable cool civility. It was such a contrast to the passionate nature he had revealed the day he had kissed her in this very place. Certainly at this moment it was impossible to reconcile the two sides of his character, if indeed there were not many more. In confusion, she rubbed her hand over her suddenly aching temples.

Lord Murray viewed Phoebe's action with a real concern for her well-being. "I must insist you return to the castle with me. I would not wish to incur young Atwood's wrath by returning you to London ill," he added, deliberately introducing the name of her betrothed to remind himself to have a care.

"Wilfred?" Phoebe questioned, wondering what Lord Murray was talking about. A mortifying possibility leapt into her mind. Surely he could not be hinting that she ought to return to England and set her sights on Wilfred! She rose and walked to the edge of the rock, not wishing Lord Murray to see the hurt she was sure was evident in her eyes. She stared fixedly into the lake, her eyes fastening on the straw bonnet that floated below. The kelpies had certainly not helped her much by conjuring up Lord Murray, if indeed they had, Phoebe thought sorrowfully.

"Miss Hartwell—"

"I told you I am fine," Phoebe interrupted without turning around. "And I am sure Wilfred will be satisfied with my condition when I return to London, whatever it may be. Please do not concern yourself for me."

Although she could not see him, Phoebe sensed Lord Murray had stepped closer and was standing right behind her. She wished desperately he would go away before she broke down, and kept her eyes fastened on the bonnet, feeling as long as she did so she could control her tears. Suddenly there was a flash under the water and the bonnet vanished abruptly, as though it had been pulled underneath the surface by an unseen hand. Startled, Phoebe jumped, and then struggled to regain her balance as her boot slipped on the wet surface of the rock. She would have fallen but for Lord Murray's strong hands grasping her shoulders and holding her firmly upright.

When Phoebe had managed to steady herself, instead of letting loose his hold upon her, Lord Murray turned her round and tipped her head up so her eyes met his. A feeling of intense yearning overwhelmed Phoebe, and she knew in that moment that she could not just walk away from Castle Abermaise without trying one last time to break the barrier that had come between her and Lord Murray. Celeste was right. She could not know what he really felt unless she asked. And what was the risk of lost pride against the prospect of losing the man she loved forever?

"Lor—" Phoebe began, but her speech was cut off as Lord Murray abruptly pulled her against his chest and silenced her lips by covering them with his in a passionate kiss. At the familiar feel of his lips upon hers Phoebe knew that she had not imagined the first kiss. But wonderful as that first had been, this one was even more so. The lips that had been soft and gentle were now hard and demanding, telling Phoebe she belonged to him, and insisting she admit the truth and submit. Phoebe readily complied, her response causing Lord Murray to hold her tighter and closer, as if they could melt into each other's very souls.

Phoebe became unaware of how much time passed as they stood embracing in their precarious position on the rock overhanging the lake, unaware and uncaring of any danger. She would have willingly stayed there in his arms forever, but finally he lifted his head from hers.

"I know you are still betrothed to Wilfred Atwood, but you care for me," he said, his voice raw with emotion. "You must break it off. Whatever you may feel you owe him, that will be more merciful in the end than marrying him when you love me."

"Wilfred?" Phoebe repeated, so bemused from the kiss that her mind only vaguely registered the name. Then the meaning of his other words became clear and her full faculties returned. "I'm not engaged to Wilfred, and never was. Wherever did you get such an idea?" she asked in astonishment, trying to step back. Lord Murray prevented her backing off the rock and led her to a safe seat.

"Why, from Miss Atwood," he answered Phoebe's question as he seated himself beside her. "She told me of your secret betrothal."

"I have *never* been engaged to Wilfred," Phoebe protested. "We are just good friends. How could Olivia have told such a tale, and how could you have believed it, knowing her?" she asked reproachfully.

"Olivia's news only supported what I had seen with my own eyes," Lord Murray said, hope springing alive that Phoebe had denied his worst fear. He told her of his seeing the kiss at the card party, and how her participation in the race had seemed to suggest that she and Atwood had had an understanding. "I had never really wanted to offer for Miss Laurence, but as a gentleman of honour I could not cut out Atwood for your affections. Then when you and Miss Laurence came to the Highlands, I knew immediately that Miss Laurence would never suit. I cannot tell you of my relief when Miss Laurence transferred her affections to Miles, for I sensed that you had come to care for me and that given enough time together I could persuade you to end your betrothal. But then Atwood arrived and the two of you seemed thick as thieves. After that everything seemed to fall apart."

"So that was it," Phoebe said, "and I thought you were either angry with me for breaking the unwritten Scottish code of hospitality, or that you had discovered I had no fortune."

"Foolish girl," he said, reaching up to smooth the wind-blown curls from her face. "I told you I did not hold you to blame for their departure, and as for your having no fortune, I have always known that and never cared. Don't you understand that I *love* you, my red-haired Scottish lass, and that I would want to marry you had you only the clothes upon your back?"

Phoebe felt herself blush at the strong emotion evident in Lord Murray's voice. Seeing her confusion, he smiled and drew her close, kissing her again, tenderly this time. Phoebe thrilled to his gentle touch and relaxed into the warmth of his body. They sat in a close embrace until the sun burned off the last of the morning mist.

"I think we had best go back or the others will think we have fallen into the loch," Lord Murray said at last, reluctantly rising and pulling Phoebe to her feet.

Reminded of the existence of others, Phoebe looked anxiously to see where the gillie was, but for the first time ever, the faithful shadow was nowhere to be seen.

"I rather suspect he has gone ahead to tell the others the news," Lord Murray commented with a grin, correctly interpreting Phoebe's furtive glances.

Phoebe laughed self-consciously and Lord Murray took her hand in his as they began to descend the path. A wonderful sense of peace and happiness filled Phoebe's heart as they walked slowly down. No longer did she dread the coming day, for now Lord Murray would be accompanying the party as well as Lord Huntsford. She and Celeste had both found their Scottish lords, as her young friend had predicted that day in London so long ago.

As Phoebe and Lord Murray neared the castle, they heard the skirl of bagpipes, and Phoebe could make out the figure of the piper as he marched slowly back and forth before the entrance of the castle.

"What is that Dinsmore is playing?" Phoebe asked her lord, liking the joyful sound of the music. "I haven't heard him play that tune before."

"That," Lord Murray said, stopping in the middle of the path and bending down to kiss Phoebe's cheek, "is the wedding march of the Murrays."

Harlequin Regency Romance™

COMING NEXT MONTH

#45 THE WILLFUL LADY by Eva Rutland
Miss Amelia Allen thought her troubles were over
when she inherited a modest fortune from her recently
deceased uncle. She was quickly to learn that her
troubles had only just begun when Guy Grosvenor,
the Duke of Winston, had been appointed her trustee.
The insufferable peacock had previously made it plain
as a pikestaff that he would have her for his mistress
and Amelia had long since decided that she would
rather turn up her toes than submit to such an
odious fate!

#46 LADY ELMIRA'S EMERALD by Winifred Witton
Viscount Oakfort had been cooling his heels in
London waiting for his childhood sweetheart, Lady
Imogen Remlow, to come of age. He had always
assumed they would be married and was quite
unprepared for her rejection. It seemed she had
become betrothed to a poet, more romantic than
Byron, compared to whom George was a dull dog.
But when Imogen loses the emerald pendant
belonging to the viscount's mother, she is soon to
learn that George is anything but dull and she must
cudgel her brains for a way to win his affections
once more.

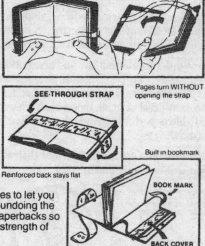